LORNA J

Ann L. Mann

ARTHUR H. STOCKWELL LTD.
Elms Court   Ilfracombe   Devon
Established 1898

©*Ann L. Mann, 1999*
First published in Great Britain, 1999
All rights reserved.
No part of this publication may be reproduced or transmitted in any form or by any means, electronic or mechanical, including photocopy, recording, or any information storage and retrieval system, without permission in writing from the copyright holder.

British Library Cataloguing-in-Publication Data.
A catalogue record for this book is available from the British Library.

ISBN 0 7223 3246-7
Printed in Great Britain by
Arthur H. Stockwell Ltd.
Elms Court   Ilfracombe
Devon

*This is an entirely fictional story,
and no conscious attempt has been made
to accurately record or recreate
any real-life events.*

Contents

Chapter 1	7
Chapter 2	10
Chapter 3	15
Chapter 4	18
Chapter 5	26
Chapter 6	33
Chapter 7	39
Chapter 8	46
Chapter 9	53
Chapter 10	59
Chapter 11	64
Chapter 12	66
Chapter 13	71
Chapter 14	74
Chapter 15	78
Chapter 16	82
Chapter 17	87
Chapter 18	90

Chapter 1

Lorna Jean sat on the green leather seat and shivered. 'It must be delayed shock,' she thought as she glanced at her watch. Almost one o'clock. She willed the tears not to spill out of her eyes for this should have been her wedding day.

Inside the art gallery, arty types, unkempt and unwashed drifted past her seat, enjoying the modern art show and looking forward to the cheap meal in the subsidized restaurant.

"What do you think of it?" An older lady, white haired and beautifully dressed, joined her on the seat and pointed to a very modern picture which Lorna Jean in her distressed state had failed to notice. "It seems to be attracting a lot of attention," she said for the sake of making conversation.

"Yes, but who would buy it?" It was a good question.

"My son painted it," she explained and Lorna Jean was thankful not to have said that it looked like nonsense to her.

"You must be very proud of him." Her dark eyes were sympathetic as she pushed her thick russet hair aside to get a better view.

They sat silent for a while then Lorna Jean stood up, reached for her straw handbag and said, "I'm off for a bite of lunch."

"Do you mind if I join you?" The woman's voice had a sad pleading tone.

Over the chicken salad they had both chosen, Lorna Jean asked "Did you go to the cheese and wine party they had for the opening of the exhibition?"

A shadow passed over the woman's worn face. "I wasn't asked. Charlie had already left home, and since my husband died, we've completely lost touch. I read about the picture in the local paper. I run a bed and breakfast establishment and since this is my playtime, I thought I'd better have a look."

"You are the very woman to help me." Lorna Jean was rummaging in her handbag and finally drew out the list of bed and breakfast accommodation she had collected from the tourist board.

The woman read it over. "You'd be quite safe in any of these houses," she said reassuringly, "but if you don't mind an attic bedroom you could have the one room I have vacant." There was an anxious expression on her face as she drew back her tinted fair hair with a hand that was heavy with diamonds.

The bills paid, they made for the car park, having first collected Lorna Jean's suitcase from the left-luggage office. It was the one she had bought for her honeymoon.

The busy streets were soon left behind and they came to a small cul-de-sac at the centre of which was an old cottage with an apple tree in the garden.

"Here we are." Dorothy McGregor jumped out and unloaded the suitcase. It's a bit away from the main centre but the bus service is good and you have the sea view of the Firth of Forth."

"Great!" A sense of security was restored in Lorna Jean. She had been so relieved to leave home with all the trauma of the last two weeks.

"Dinner is at six-thirty" Dorothy said.

So she paid for a week's lodgings and walked down the twisty path to a quiet village street where she spotted a phone box. With her heart beating wildly she dialled her parents' number.

Her father answered, his voice gruff.

"Before the money runs out, will you take the address and phone number of the lodgings." Her voice was breathless as she repeated it twice. "Everything alright at that end?" she asked.

"Yes!" he said and banged down the receiver.

To pass the time before dinner, she walked. It was the only way she could fight the depression that was threatening to engulf her. Anyone seeing her tall slim figure, the flawless complexion and the friendly smile, would surely have been puzzled by Crawford's phone call to cancel the wedding at ten days' notice. There had been no quarrel, no explanation; he just phoned then disappeared leaving his mother, a widow, in a state of shock and Lorna Jean's parents to cope with the return of the presents, give the wedding dress to charity and the cake to the old folks' home.

Crawford's minister had said it was just pre-wedding nerves. It happened all the time. He'd be back.

Lorna Jean's minister said that a man who could treat people like that was well out of her life and he prayed that her future would be blessed.

By half past five she was exhausted. The traffic in the city was horrific. There was a limit to the shops she could browse in and the coffee she could drink, so when the local bus stopped to pick up passengers, she struggled aboard and was at Dorothy's house in ten minutes.

A Canadian couple were in the sitting room, also an English couple who were visiting their student son. Lorna Jean joined them and they all chatted until the maid gonged for dinner.

The Canadians had booked for a concert and the other couple were making a surprise visit to their son's flat. "He's probably eating baked beans from the tin," his mother said sadly.

The maid lived out, so Dorothy joined Lorna Jean in the lounge. "What does your fiancé do?" Dorothy was admiring the sparkling engagement ring on her lodger's finger.

There was a painful silence, then Lorna Jean sobbed out the story.

Dorothy gasped. "Your wedding day." She looked at the tear-stained face and was aghast that any parent could let this lovely girl be alone on such a tragic day. "Was there a quarrel?"

"No — he just jilted me." Lorna Jean was wiping her eyes.

Dorothy patted her arm. "All I can say is that you have had a lucky escape."

Chapter 2

She woke up next morning with the sun's rays streaming in the window and Dorothy at her bedside with a breakfast tray. "I just let you sleep on," she explained. "This is my day to help out with the meals for the charity drive. You can join me if you want, and I'll leave you afterwards to do your own thing."

They set out an hour later, and the time passed pleasantly. Everyone was friendly and flushed with 'do-gooding'. She washed and stacked dishes, took her turn at the cash desk, then left at the same time as Dorothy, who had to get back to the guests.

"I'll walk down the Royal Mile," she said "and I'll see you after dinner."

There was something in the old buildings that was strangely reassuring. People had lived here, suffered and overcome worse than she had.

She went into the Museum of Childhood — all the old-fashioned foods and medicines, the lovely toys and the wonder expressed on the faces of a school party enjoying the experience in the company of an older teacher.

Back at Dorothy's, the four guests were back.

"How was the baked bean eater?" she asked his mother, and the father laughed.

"Worse than we feared. Three boys, piles of dirty clothes, no dishes washed, but they were all so happy, so who were we to complain!"

The Canadians were loving Edinburgh. "It's so civilized," they assured her.

She went early to bed and slept better than she had done for weeks.

Next morning after the other guests had departed, Dorothy, a concerned look on her face, asked "What do you intend to do with your future?"

It was a loaded question. Before the jilting, Lorna Jean had taught in the local school. There had been a presentation party on the last day of term. "I'm looking forward to you coming back as a married lady, the school needs you," the headmistress had said.

"I just don't know what to do. I taught in a school but I don't fancy going back to face the teachers in the staff room."

"Why don't you phone the education officer. I'm sure they will understand and arrange some sort of transfer for you."

"I think I'll write. Would you mind if I stayed on here until I get things sorted out?"

"As long as it takes. I think we are good for each other." Dorothy was smiling. "It's almost like finding the daughter I never had."

So the letter was sent.

The reply came promptly. Could she interview the director of education the following Monday at 2.30 p.m., which gave her ample time to go by train. Her mother had phoned and approved of her plan. Everything was falling into place. She dressed carefully for the interview, had a new hairdo and on being called into the office of the great man, found he already knew her story.

He started to leaf among a pile of papers. "I take it you are looking for a fresh start?"

He was a fatherly type and put Lorna Jean at her ease.

"Ah, here it is," he said, pushing his glasses to the top of his head. "There's a vacancy for a one-teacher school in the Western Isles. Not everybody's idea of the good life, but it could be the solution in your present circumstances."

So it came about, that on the last Tuesday in August, when the heather was purple on the hills, Lorna Jean sat in an observation coach and feasted her eyes on the glorious scenery that flashed past as the train covered the miles that lay between Glasgow and Oban. As the distance lessened, her heart grew lighter and a huge weight lifted from her shoulders. The small boat that was riding the harbour waves would be the one that would take her to the new life.

She sat on her suitcase until the boat's owner came down the landing stage and said, "Och, I'm thinking you'll be the new teacher; I'm Lachie."

He tossed the suitcase aboard, hitched up the collar of his thick, brown, homespun jersey, and with a tug of the outboard motor, Lorna Jean was on her way.

A battered car was bumping its way over the rough road at right angles to the landing stage where Lachie was tying up the boat.

"That's auld Jimsie," he explained as he helped Lorna Jean ashore, and followed her up the shingly beach to stow her suitcase in the boot of the battered car. "Jimsie will drive you to Katrina's cottage." He shouted "It's the new teacher," and was off down to the boat. Time was money.

Jimsie, with some difficulty, forced open the passenger door. "Och, it's a real bugger for sticking," he explained as the new teacher was hit by the smell of fish which rose from the seat.

Then he seized the wheel and shot off, scattering six sheep, two dogs, a goat and an interested small boy who had come to inspect the new teacher. "I think Katrina was worrying about you being from yon Glasco but you look alright to me," Jimsie conceded. "Mind you, it's a place I would not be wanting to see my boys go to."

Before Lorna Jean could answer, he shot forward along the bumpy road and screamed to a halt at a picturesque ruin of a cottage where a beautiful, dark-haired woman stood smiling on the front step.

"You'll be needing a cup of tea," she said to Lorna Jean who was standing in the uncut grass while Jimsie unloaded the suitcase.

The room they entered was warm from the peat fire which scented the atmosphere and lit up the brasses and the bubbling kettle. There was a small scullery for cooking and washing-up. The room was used for dining, relaxing and entertaining. The tea was served in large thick mugs, of the type usually sold in hand-thrown pottery shops. The scones were home baked, the butter real and the raspberry jam and double cream in the luxury class. They came in the company of oatcakes, pancakes and crowdie (a local cream cheese).

"Och, I'm thinking this will fairly set me up for the lobster run." Jimsie was belching his appreciation.

The door flew open and a young girl, with sleek blue-black hair and eyes that reflected the pale green of the sea, burst in. "Just in time for a chittering bite and a quick cuppa," she explained.

"My daughter Morveen." Katrina moved forward and said "Meet the new teacher. Morveen has just left school and goes to college in Inverness in October. She's working in the big house for the summer."

They sat companionably round the scrubbed white table.

Then Jimsie stood up. "Thanks for the hospitality, but some of us have to work," he said.

Morveen fluttered her long dark eyelashes. "Any chance of a lift to the big house?" she asked pleadingly.

"I'll have to consult my lawyer," Jimsie assured her as he winked at Lorna Jean.

"See you Sunday" Morveen said as she kissed her mother.

"Och, she's the light of my life." The mother sighed as the door swung shut. "She is all I have left of the handsome American sailor who loved me and left me. I keep thinking he'll be back."

"Could be," Lorna Jean said, although she didn't believe it for one split second.

The bedrooms were to the back of the house, sheltered from the wild winds by the sheer cliff where sheep grazed.

"I hope they don't disturb you," Katrina worried.

"Nothing will disturb me," her lodger assured her and she was right.

At the first bleat, she reached for her watch — it was time for breakfast.

"Is there a phone?" she asked.

"There's one outside the general store. You'd better use it now as there are always queues in the evenings."

"That's great, I'll phone home now on my way to inspect the school." She couldn't wait to tell her parents that she had arrived safely and was so happy to be on the island.

Chapter 3

Irenie Stuart put her feet up on the padded stool and let Lorna Jean's father answer the phone. She was physically and mentally at the end of her tether. So traumatic had the cancelled wedding been, she felt it could be years before she would be able to face the world.

He came into the kitchen, tall and handsome, his thick, dark hair neat, his suit well pressed. Jack Stuart's seafaring training had made everything in his life well ordered and shipshape. "That was our daughter. She's fine, settling in nicely."

"Bully for her," his wife said, bitterness in her voice as she recalled the aftermath of Crawford's phone call.

"I'm going out."

His wife sighed. "Does that mean you won't be in for tea?"

"No! I'm having it out. Everything's done and I feel I've spent too much of my shore leave with nothing to show for it."

"Please yourself," she sighed and closed her eyes.

He had just gone when the phone rang again. It was Mrs Martin, Crawford's mother. "Just to say Crawford phoned from London. He's safe and well."

"That's more than we are," Irenie snapped. "Safe and well," she fumed. "Who the hell does she think she's kidding," she muttered to herself. It was all over the town that her precious son was being pursued by a local couple whose daughter was heavily pregnant.

The doorbell rang and there on the step was the Rev. J. Clark.

"Just to check on how things are going." He was settling in Jack's armchair as Irenie hurried to the kitchen to make tea.

"Great!" she called from the kitchen. "We've just had a phone call. She's landed the post of head teacher in a western island school and she is there to prepare for the new term."

"I told you it would turn out for the best." He was reaching out for a cream cake to take the wetness off the tea. "How are you going to fill in your time now that Lorna Jean is away and the boys going back to college?"

"I haven't had time to make plans."

"I was wondering if you could help us with the women's clubs. We're short of organizers."

Irenie actually smiled. "I'll be delighted," she assured him.

Meanwhile, down at the 'Hole in the Wall', the barmaid leant on the counter and listened to Jack Stuart's tales of the sea. "It must be great to be so well travelled." She threw back her long blonde hair and opened her blue eyes wide in admiration.

"It really is the life," Jack assured her. "I could get you a great job as a stewardess and we could sail the seven seas making whoopee."

"My, you're an awful man." Celia pulled his fifth pint and matched it with a chaser of whisky.

"A big ham sandwich would go down a treat," Jack assured her.

"For you, anything," she said as she sent the order down the blower. "Heard your daughter was getting married," Celia said to change the subject.

"Oh, for God's sake, don't mention that."

"Why?"

"The blasted bridegroom never turned up — did a bunk ten days before the ceremony." He was beating the counter with his glass, his face purple, the veins swollen. The regulars had stopped drinking to listen.

Celia's eyes were popping with disbelief as she pushed the plate of sandwiches towards him.

"Lord Almighty, it was terrible — just phoned and

cancelled the whole bloody lot." He held his empty glass out for a refill and went on. "There were dresses for the women, kilts for the men and my ceremonial naval uniform was out of the mothballs."

"That was terrible." Celia was really sympathetic.

"And a ruddy great cake that had to be given to the old folks' home. Cost a mint of my money." He swayed on his stool to survey the other drinkers who had suspended all conversation to soak up the tragic tale. He put down the last empty glass narrowly missing the counter. "Phone for a taxi, Celia love," he pleaded.

"You're getting worse," Celia said as two willing cronies offered to get him home.

Irenie knew what to expect when she heard the loud voices and the scuffles on the stairs. She had seen it all before. Her two young sons, home for the wedding, rushed to the spare bedroom and prepared the couch kept for situations like this. She reached for her purse to pay the taxi fare. It was the end of a blighted shore leave. The only bright thought was that he would sail out on tomorrow's tide and on Friday the shipping agent's cheque would be behind the door.

He appeared at lunch time all spruced up and ready to go. The two boys accepted a fiver each in the spirit it was offered, and if Irenie had any thought that her gift of a silver bracelet had been bought with someone else in mind, she gave no clue. "Thank you," she said, kissing him softly on the cheek. "I'll wear it to the women's club on Wednesdays."

Chapter 4

"You'll be coming to the party on Saturday?"

Lorna Jean was sipping a glass of white wine in the company of the mobile hairdresser who had called to do Katrina's hair.

"But I haven't been asked to a party."

"Neither have I or anyone else for that matter. You just go. It's called Highland Hospitality. It's the laird's turn on Saturday. It's a great idea."

As she set Lorna Jean's hair in a very flattering style, the hairdresser told her how she had come to the island. "I met Rory when I flew into Palma, Majorca with a girlfriend from London. We were together for most of the holiday. 'You should come to my island and set up business,' he said. He was gorgeous and I would have gone to the ends of the earth for him. There would be no opposition and I could also do the gents' work. People would appreciate not having to go to Oban. Of course, I thought he was in love with me. How was I to know that he was a married man with a clutch of weans, as they say in this part of the world. But I never regretted the change. I bought a small cottage and had an old van fitted out with the hairdressing equipment. I'm my own boss. What more could a woman want?"

Jimsie drove Lorna Jean and Katrina to the big house where fiddles were being tuned and people were flocking into the large dining room that had been cleared for dancing.

As the band struck up, an exquisite young man with fair,

curling hair and perfect features introduced himself. "I'm Mac the art teacher," he explained as the band struck up an eightsome reel.

It was tough work but the music was inspiring. Having completed the set, he led her to a couple of chairs. "I'm really a freelance artist working two days at the school to help out with the expenses while I build up the art shop my grandfather left me last year."

Katrina was meanwhile having a deep and romantic conversation with a large, bearded man who hailed Mac. He winked at Ian who said "There's old Katrina about to make another of her romantic mistakes."

The band tempo changed and a handsome, older man held out his hand to Lorna Jean. "Come on, my dear," he said in a cultivated English accent, "let's show them how good we can be in this lovely Scottish waltz."

He was a joy to dance with and when the waltz was over, he said, "Let's go to the buffet. I've been out fishing all day and I'm starving." It was when he said, "I must be the only man in the room eating his own food," that it dawned on her that this must be the laird.

"I'm the new teacher." She accepted the glass of white wine to go with the food he had piled on her plate. "I've just newly arrived and have you to thank for the chance to meet the islanders."

He gazed into his glass. "It was my late wife's idea. After she died, all sorts of people offered to help if I provided the house, which is the largest on the island." He glanced at the diamond ring sparkling on her engagement finger. "What have you done with the boyfriend?" he asked.

"He's not in my life any more. As a matter of fact, he walked out on me ten days before the wedding. That's why I'm here. I just wear the ring to keep the wolves away." She was laughing for the first time in weeks.

"You'll like it here and being so close to Oban helps keep you in touch with the outside world. By the way, there's a classical concert over there next Saturday night. If you would care to join me, I'd be very happy. We've both had harrowing experiences, so a night out would cheer us up. I'll meet you at the jetty at six o'clock. The next dance is a progressive barn dance. We'll start it off and you'll get a chance to meet all the talent."

And she did meet them — the minister, the school janitor, two fishing boat owners, a randy farmer and an American landowner.

She slipped out before the next dance. All she wanted was to cosy down alone in her comfortable bed and read the new paperback she had bought in Glasgow.

Sleep overtook her. The book slid to the floor and the next thing she knew Katrina was pounding on the bedroom door.

"If you're going to church with me you'd better hurry."

'Church! My God, that's all I need,' she thought as she scrambled into her clothes.

"My, but you had a great time last night." Katrina sounded envious.

"You looked as if you were doing alright yourself."

"Maybe so" Katrina agreed, "but it's the keeping them pinned down that I find so difficult."

Lorna Jean looked down at her hand. In the rush to get dressed, she had left her engagement ring on the dressing table. She took it as a sign. From that day on she would keep it in her purse. A talisman if she was ever short of money, and the first step to a new life.

The little church on the hill that overlooked the harbour was full of worshippers. All the drunk-crazed characters from the night before were there hung over, praying in the bosom of their families.

"We're going to Meg's for a hand-round lunch," Katrina announced as they came down the church steps. "She's great at reading the crystal."

"Is she the seventh daughter of the seventh daughter?" Lorna Jean was laughing and thinking it was a queer way to spend a Sunday afternoon.

Meg lived with her brother Roddy in what had once been her father's fisherman's cottage. "Roddy's not back yet, so we'll get the fortunes under control first," Meg said as she swept two large ginger cats from the couch and invited her guests to sit down.

She put the crystal ball on a small card table and addressed Lorna Jean. "Och, my, but there has been some terrible trouble and disappointment in your life. A fair-haired man let you down. That's all in the past now and soon you'll meet your true love. You'll always have money and interesting work and . . . !!"

The speil was interrupted when a tall, bearded man burst into the room. "Will you stop all that heathenish carry on," he yelled. "This is the Sabbath day." He turned his far-seeking dark blue eyes on Lorna Jean as Meg rushed to the kitchen to serve up the steak pie. "Surely an educated woman like yourself would no be believing such stupid nonsense."

As they made their way back to Katrina's cottage, Lorna Jean was amazed to find that Sunday evening on the island did not fill her with dread of Monday morning as was the case in the city school situation.

And she was right. The children, when she met them, were delightful. Fourteen in number, they ranged in ages from a small five-year-old, clinging to his mother's hand, to three girls who would go to the secondary school on the mainland the next year. It was lovely to have the variety of age learning instead of listening to the same old reading book repeated thirty-two times.

So, what with making up the register, tempting James, the five-year-old, with Plasticine, building blocks and painting on news-sheets while the others got on with their work, it was lunch break before she had time to be bored.

"You've been a very clever boy," she said to James. "Your mummy's waiting in the cloakroom to take you home."

He burst into tears. "I don't want to go home," he sobbed.

"That's praise for you." His mother was laughing as she fastened his coat.

The bell shrilled and the pupils started moving. A very small woman appeared from nowhere. "It's your dinner break, Miss Stuart," she said officiously. "I take over now. Leave everything to me."

As the new head teacher opened the morning newspaper and popped it against the milk jug, she put up a silent prayer of thanks to the director of education who had steered her away from crowded classrooms.

She had just finished the excellent lunch when the little woman popped her head round the door. "I have to tell you, Miss Stuart, that we pay for our share of the tea, biscuits and the paper at the beginning of every month. And, oh, you will need a cup. Feel free to use mine till you get your own. I'm Miss Kerr, by the way. I help out at lunch time and am in charge of the school bus mornings and afternoons. I've heard that they all call me 'Wee Maggie' behind my back."

Lorna Jean felt she should put this interfering wee busybody in her place, but decided against it. Life was too short.

The afternoon flew past. Having made sure that everyone was on the school bus, she left the building to the janitor and the cleaner and stepped into the soft sunshine. She was suffering from anticlimax.

The Oban boat left at four-thirty. "I've got to get some things over at the mainland, but I'll be back for supper," she informed Katrina who was hanging sheets up to dry. "Anything you want?"

"A shop-made apple tart!"

The town still had a holiday air. She bought an expensive cup and saucer and dismissed the wedding present tea set that her mother had sent back.

The bookshop was not too busy and browsing was a real pleasure. Soon she had bought two books, a small box of paints, a sketch pad and a paintbrush. After she had put the purchases in a new shopping bag that had caught her fancy, she paused to study the window display of a house-selling agency. There in the very centre was a *For Sale* notice. "I don't believe this," she said to herself as she read the description of a two-roomed cottage for sale on the island.

She opened the office door and a young salesman sprang to life. "Can I help you?"

"I've just come to the island as the head teacher and I might be interested in the cottage for sale."

He was no time in telling her the asking price and the monthly mortgage which was cheaper than the lodgings. "I can give you the phone number of the owner's son who lives locally. His mother has gone to be with her daughter in Skye."

Armed with the information and flushed with excitement, she bought some delicious fish and chips and caught the five-thirty ferry back. She spent the rest of the evening sharing the reheated fish supper and shop apple cake with Katrina.

"If you buy that wee house, we'll be neighbours," Katrina said, not worried about losing her lodger. She could now have her new boyfriend in if Lorna Jean was not staying. He had been hinting at the idea for some time. It could all be a matter of fate, she decided.

The owner's son came over with the keys to let her view the cottage. It was everything she had ever wanted. She couldn't wait to contact the lawyer and put in the offer. He was young and eager and good looking, which was light relief after being cooped up with a class full of children all day.

"I'm sure they'll accept your offer," he said. "I know they are keen to get it off their hands." He assured her he'd be in touch as soon as possible.

She left his office and went to the hotel to phone home.

"Are you sure you're doing the right thing?" It was her mother who answered, pouring cold water on her plans.

'Oh God,' she thought, as she put down the receiver. 'Nobody trusts a jilted woman to get things right,' she thought as she ordered a steakburger and a quick drink and went for the boat.

The laird, on his way home from the cattle market, hailed her and she told him the news. "That's a great chance," he assured her. "You have a steady income and stone and lime is the best investment. I can assure you that the cottage is in very good order. See you Saturday" he reminded her as they walked home.

Charlie, the son of the owner, handed in the keys to the school. All his mother's possessions had been removed. He said he was sad to see what had been his birthplace going to a complete stranger, but he had a wife and four children, so he was renting a large house from the estate.

An empty house to put her stamp on was exactly what Lorna Jean was craving for, so she lost no time in putting in an offer.

"I'm almost there," she assured the laird when he called for her on the Saturday.

The concert was wonderful, the only snag being that John, the laird, was staying overnight with friends, so Lorna Jean had to come back with a group of islanders who had been over to see a film. She was glad of their friendly conversation and felt part of the scene.

It was all of ten days before the lawyer phoned the school. "Good news," he said. "Your offer has been accepted."

It was the best possible news. The laird — she was now calling him John — pointed out that even if she was not always teaching on the island, the cottage would make a great holiday home.

The Saturday morning she went to the lawyers to finalize the deal, was one of the best in her life. She had a house with no rising damp because a damp course had been put in. The kitchen-cum-living room was surprisingly spacious and the large walk-in cupboard in the hall had been converted to a shower room. Best of all, there was electricity.

"It's a great wee house," Katrina assured her, when the keys had been handed over and they started exploring. "Mrs Robertson was terribly house-proud. Hardly a week went by without her having something done. What a pity she was crippled in an accident and couldn't live on her own any more."

The painter from the laird's estate would do the walls to earn himself extra money. Country cream with one tangerine wall for the big room. Forest green and pale pink for the bedroom. She had found blue and white wallpaper for the kitchen, which was very small, and could do with cheering up. Her father, who had not got round to buying a wedding present, was supplying the carpets. Her mother bought the bed on the strength of being asked to stay, which was fine as there would be a bed couch in the big room.

She had the house-warming five weeks later and let it be known that from then on it would be open house.

Her mother came over for the weekend and slept in the bed while her daughter dossed down on the sofa. "I could fair do with a wee house like this," she said wistfully.

But the most constant visitor was Mac, the art teacher. Having painted two beautiful pictures to set off the tangerine wall, he took to dropping in at all times.

"Have you made up your mind between Mac and the laird?" Katrina teased as they walked home from church.

Lorna Jean laughed. "Well, you know how it is with the choice of two men. You don't really love either of them. Mind you, in my case I have decided to be a sinister spinster."

"Deil the fear of it," said Katrina.

They were on their way to Lorna Jean's cottage. She had left a cold buffet. Meg had gone on ahead to pack lunch for Roddy to take out on a fishing trip with his friends.

"This is such a comfortable house," Katrina said as she lay back on the couch and sipped a glass of red wine.

The sun's rays had caught the picture Mac had painted and the crystal vase which held the brightly-coloured flowers added a touch of class to the room.

"If I could earn enough to have all this I wouldn't see a man in my road," Katrina said as Meg joined them.

Chapter 5

It was rapidly approaching half term when Lorna Jean's newly-installed phone rang. It was Myra Clark who had been a college friend and taught languages in a city school. "I got your phone number from your mum" she said. "Are you doing anything over the holidays?"

"Not really." Lorna Jean was intrigued.

"It's just that I'm taking a school party to Rome and Sorrento. One of the teachers has taken ill and I'm looking for someone to take her place. I wondered if you could help me out?"

"I'd love to."

"Great! I'll send you all the documents and joining instructions. And please, please don't change your mind."

"I won't."

So she went home that weekend to visit her mother and collect her passport.

Her mother was delighted. "That solves my problem." She was actually smiling. "The church women's club are having a Lake District holiday at that time. The boys are going camping, so if you'd come for the school holiday, I'd have worried about you being alone in the house."

"Oh, good." Lorna Jean resisted the temptation of telling her mother that she'd never had any intention of coming at that time.

So it was back to the island to pack the bag and join the happy travellers in Glasgow.

Myra was on the top bunk of the compartment they shared on the sleeper. "How come you ended up teaching on an island?" she asked Lorna Jean. "The last I heard of you, a marriage had been arranged."

"It's a long story," said Lorna Jean, and told her.

"You're better without him."

"I realize that." Lorna Jean was yawning, lulled by the motion of the train.

The next thing she knew, the steward was knocking on the door to serve the morning coffee.

The plane from London touched down and soon they were loaded onto a travel coach which took them to Rome's main rail station entrance to meet another school party who never turned up because the train had been delayed.

The courier, a handsome but temperamental Italian, went berserk.

"Why don't you take us to the hotel and go back for the others?" Myra asked reasonably.

This drew from Roberto a torrent of Italian and a prima donna performance before he decided to do just that.

The hotel was sheer luxury. "Look at the bath!" Myra, who was sharing the magnificent twin room with Lorna Jean had opened a door to reveal a sunken marble bath. "You could swim in that," she pointed out as they went to check on the students who were settling in with noisy excitement.

"Dinner is at seven." The courier was reading table numbers from a lengthy list. "I will not be escorting you in Rome. You'll be free to explore by yourselves."

Myra divided the pupils into groups each supervised by two teachers.

Next morning they booked a city tour.

"That way you'll see it all and then you'll have time to go back to any part you would like to walk about in."

"It's not the least like what I thought it would be" Lorna Jean said to Myra as the coach crawled through the traffic. "I pictured it more crowded and built up — not so many green spaces."

The guide was pointing out the Spanish Steps and telling them of an English tearoom.

But Myra rejected that idea. "Let's find an Italian outdoor café where we can have a snack and sit at the pavement tables and watch the world go by."

There was one not far from where the tour ended. As they waited for the burgers and soft drinks, they watched a romantically dressed traffic policeman direct the lines of cars that were rolling into the city. He stood on top of a high platform, drunk with power.

Then, from the pavement, came the excited shouting of a group of tourists hailing the policeman who recognised them, obviously friends from his home village.

Leaving the traffic to fend for itself, with outbreaks of road rage and the sounding of horns, he came down from his perch to be hugged and kissed and admired by his friends.

Just as a revolution was about to break out, he tore himself free, remounted his observation post and resumed directing the traffic as if nothing had happened.

The hotel dinner was superb but everyone was so travel weary that an early night was the first priority. Nobody was interested in the nightlife.

Lorna Jean, having slept dreamlessly, woke to the shafts of bright Italian sunshine already in the room. She took a quick bath before she woke Myra, who was in danger of oversleeping and missing breakfast.

Immediately afterwards, they were on their way to Sorrento. The suitcases were still in the coach, so it was only a matter of packing the overnight bags.

At breakfast, Roberto prowled like some sleep-starved avenger. His life was filled with lists and timetables and carefree humans hellbent on wrecking his plans.

"This is all going so well," Myra said as if she had feared some terrible incident.

The Amalfi drive to Sorrento was one of spectacular beauty. The road was high above a sea of dazzling blue and all the houses that clung to the cliffs were owned by the rich and famous.

"Does this remind you of your highland home?" Myra asked Lorna Jean.

"No," she replied, "but home is where the heart is."

The Sorrento hotel was built high on a hill overlooking the Bay of Naples. On the road leading to the entrance was a small house and workshop where an extended family made beautiful inlaid wooden musical boxes and small three-legged work boxes which played 'Back to Sorrento' when you raised the lid.

Lorna Jean wandered down the hill, while Myra took charge of overseeing the pupils unpack. She was due time off and wanted a souvenir for her new home.

"My word, the Italians are so efficient," Myra said, promising herself a visit later after dinner. "The notice said they'd be open until ten o'clock."

The courier came into the dining room and shouted, "Tomorrow Vesuvius — breakfast at seven-thirty. The volcano has been misbehaving" he said in a tone calculated to leave everyone feeling vulnerable.

The journey next day was dull and without the beauty of Sorrento. When Roberto announced they were going up to the volcano by chair lift, the pupils cheered. Lorna Jean had never been on a chair lift, so she felt no fear when she fastened the chain on the one next to Myra. It was only when they gathered height and speed and the surrounding countryside stretched beneath her, that she lost her nerve and started to scream. In her panic, she pulled at the safety chain threatening to jump off.

"Don't dare." Myra leant forward to prevent her.

She was still screaming hysterically when they reached the top. "Jump," shouted Myra as she pulled her off.

They staggered to a small stall selling thick black coffee in tiny cups. The whole scene was obscured by the sulphur that was belching from the crater.

The coffee restored them somewhat and they were able to fight their way through the sulphur clouds to check that the pupils were safely with the guide. They joined the party but the guide's words were lost on Lorna Jean. All her worry was focused on her fear of the downward chair lift.

The lecture over, they saw their party safely aboard; boys and girls holding hands, lost in the romance of the situation.

"Fasten the chain and close your eyes." Myra's voice was teacherish.

Lorna Jean was fine until something hit her foot.

"Don't worry, it's only a tree top," but her friend was still whimpering when they hit the ground.

The next day was a romantic boat journey to the isle of Capri.

"Lovely." Lorna Jean had no worries. It would just be like home with lots of sunshine added. But she reckoned without the Mediterranean. When the storm hit them everybody was ordered below deck. It was a sick making expedition.

Eventually, they landed on the island. It really was romantic but they had to miss the visit to the blue grotto, cancelled because of the adverse weather.

"At least we've seen it." Myra, always the comforter, said as they stepped off the boat, thankful to be back to Sorrento.

It was then that the bottom pinching began. The local youths were out in full force. Their female contemporaries were all safely at home. The school party was fair game.

"Have you never seen a pair of bare legs before?" one girl asked a soulful follower. He hadn't a clue what she was talking about. His English was basic to say the least.

"Your profoseros are very severo," he complained.

The more sophisticated came on powerful motorbikes roaring along the pavement, the better to study the girls. It was all a great game for a boring evening in an area where the nightlife was only for the tourists.

Next day was the coach tour to Naples which was a different Italian picture.

Stopping on the way at a small village for morning coffee, they were swamped by mobs of ragged children galvanized into action by the spies who spotted the coach and yelled "Americanos".

"That's terrible," Myra said in disgust as they fought their way into the café. After the lovely creamy coffee and rich cakes, it made it more difficult to ignore the mob.

"Let's collect our spare small coins and scatter them on our way out," Lorna Jean suggested.

The pupils thought this a brilliant idea, and they were able to board the coach while the beggars scrambled for the money.

The town was hot, dusty and noisy. "It's much better looking at it from across the bay," they all decided.

"It's not the place I would want to build a holiday home," one of the girls added.

They left the city, glad to be away from the slums, the beggars and the oppressive heat, to pack for the next day's journey up the Amalfi drive to finish the holiday in Rome. The whole city was in a fever of excitement because the home football team were playing for the Italian cup.

"I hope the Rome team win it," Lorna Jean said as they tossed the three coins in the fountain to ensure a return to Rome. "It will make an evening to remember."

Dinner that night was hilarious. There was a television in the kitchen and waiters careered through swing doors to throw plates of delicious food on the table in order to get back to check on the team. The staff and students had no idea how things were going until they went to the lounge for coffee and heard the staff cheering and the car horns blaring. When the first lot of fireworks started to explode, the whole school party went out to celebrate. It was sheer street theatre. But tomorrow they were going home, so it was time to pack with the sounds of revelry still ringing in their ears.

"We'll miss this," Myra said as they checked that none of their charges had sneaked off.

"Still it's good to be going home," Lorna Jean said, already homesick for the island.

In the reception hall of the hotel next morning, emotional waiters were declaring undying love as the pupils piled into the airport coach. It was then that Lorna Jean discovered that she had mislaid her airport ticket.

"I'll have to keep you hostage," the exquisite ticket steward declared.

Then she remembered it was in the book she was carrying to read on the plane.

London looked drab and dull as they went on to join the sleeper for the last lap of the journey.

As they walked along the platform, there was a sound of shattering glass. Bill McNair, the maths teacher, had dropped the large straw-covered bottle he had lugged all the way from Sorrento.

"Don't let Mr McNair see you laughing," Myra warned as the wine poured out over the platform.

Chapter 6

Lorna Jean was struggling with the contents of the package that contained the three legs and the top of the Sorrento worktable, when Katrina called for coffee. For a start, the three legs did not match. "I'll have to call Alisdair the joiner," she said and started to laugh. "When I bought this, a businessman who was going home to England bought a nest of tables for his girlfriend. I hope all the legs match."

It was so lovely to be home, she thought as she sorted out the little reminders of her holiday and put them where she could recall the happy time.

"Have you seen Mac?" Katrina asked. "He said he wasn't going away, but the shop never opened, and nobody has seen him for ages."

Lorna Jean shook her head. "I sent him a postcard and expected to see him, but there's been no sign. I'll see him at school on Monday."

But once the assembly was over, there was no sign of Mac. "I'll have to mark him absent on the time sheet" Lorna Jean said and started to worry because he was paid by the hour and would lose money.

"All those artist blokes have no sense of responsibility," Wee Maggie said.

She agreed, but she had the nagging feeling that something was wrong.

"What do you think I should do?" She was having tea with

Katrina who had made a delicious fish pie and wanted someone to share it with.

"There's not much you can do until the office ask for a medical line." Katrina was serving the pie. "He may have been held up somewhere and turn up on the last boat."

"I'll see Jimsie and phone you later."

Katrina actually thought it was a great fuss about nothing.

On the way home she overtook John. "Hello!" he shouted. "How was the holiday?"

"Great! I threw three coins in the fountain. I'll go back."

"Everything alright at school?"

"Yes, except that Mac hasn't turned up and nobody seems to know where he is."

"That's funny. The shop never opened and the tourists were asking. I'll ask around and phone if I hear any news."

Roddy McLean who combined the duties of part-time policeman with voluntary duties on the lifeboat, had contacted Mac's family who had not heard from him and were worried.

Into the second week, the local newspaper on the mainland sent a reporter. Mac's parents had come over and were staying with the laird. Parties of residents searched the island. Nothing was found.

It was a wild dark night on the third week when the phone rang. It was John. "Mac is dead." His voice was unsteady. "The body was washed up on a beach two miles from Oban."

She ran to Katrina and together they sobbed.

"How could it happen?" they asked Roddy McLean.

"He took great risks with the company he kept. A lot of artists are homosexual. Maybe it was the best thing for him to go home to his maker before things got too difficult for him to handle."

That night in her lonely bed, Lorna Jean cried herself to sleep. "Why does everything I touch end in disaster?" she asked herself as she fell into a disturbed sleep.

Next day, she collected all Mac's equipment from the school's walk-in cupboard. She would store it until after the funeral.

"His mother's a widow, poor woman, and he was her only son." Katrina was wiping a tear from her eye. "Will you get someone else?" she asked.

"Oh yes, an art teacher from the mainland is coming over in a week's time. Three of the pupils are being presented for examinations and I don't have art in my degree, so there has to be a trained person."

The McDonalds came over that weekend. The husband was the teacher referred to by his wife as 'My Colin'.

Dolina McDonald took over from the moment she crossed Lorna Jean's doorstep. "We wondered if you could let us look at the school?" she said, plumping down on the best armchair as her husband stood by. "It's lovely here Colin. You'll be able to do spare-time painting."

Lorna Jean took down the keys, and somewhat reluctantly led them to the school.

"I suppose the shop will be up for sale?" Mrs McDonald had no finer feelings. She was raking in the school cupboards and assessing what was left of the requisition. "Colin will teach and I'll run the shop" she said as they walked away to get the boat. "It's something I've always wanted to do. Like us, you're not from these parts?" She had inquisitive eyes.

"No, I'm from Glasgow. I lodged in the village until the cottage was ready."

"Is it your own?"

"Yes."

Her husband, a dreamy man with a pronounced Highland accent, looked embarrassed.

"I hope you manage to buy the shop." Lorna Jean addressed her remarks to him.

"If fate has decided we should live here, everything should turn out alright," he said and sighed.

"Listen to him," Dolina said to no one in particular.

"I tell you, if that couple buy the shop and settle on the island, it will never be the same," Katrina who had come over on the boat with them declared. "If ever a man was henpecked, it's that one. That woman could rule the country."

Colin McDonald arrived two weeks later.
 Lorna Jean heaved a sigh of relief. "I was so worried about the senior pupils," she told him.
 "We'll soon catch up," he assured her "and thanks for keeping them up with the written work for the history of art. We're lodging in Oban to see how things turn out. If the wife doesn't get the shop, she'll start up something over there."

Winter on the island was magic. The snow never reached ground level but rested on the tops of the distant mountains, making the view against the dark blue of the ocean one of unforgettable beauty. The cottage was so cosy — a haven of peace after a hard day's teaching, not easy with such a range of ages and there was all the administration.
 "I get so bloody sick of all this red tape," Lorna Jean grumbled to Katrina as she pushed aside a pile of forms that had to be posted that very evening, and poured the brandy and ginger tonic her friend had such faith in as a cure for the blues.
 Katrina was having man trouble and could think of nothing else.
 "You'll be alright when the tourist season starts," Lorna Jean assured her, glad that she was fancy-free and not dependent on any man.
 It was almost a month since Lorna Jean had written to Mac's mother. 'Do come and stay if you are ever on the island,' she had suggested. She still had his things in her kitchen cupboard.

When the phone rang one evening, the woman said she was Marjorie and she was coming over to arrange for the sale of the shop.
 Lorna Jean's heart sank.
 Colin and she were rubbing along very well. He was an excellent teacher and spent a lot of extra time on the exam pupils without neglecting the younger ones.
 "Have you had any offers?"
 "Yes! The most promising one is from the wife of the new

art teacher. The living part would save her husband the stress of travelling and she's always wanted to run a business."

'You can say that again,' Lorna Jean thought as she arranged to have Marjorie in the bedroom. "It's alright," she assured her. "The living room couch bed is very comfortable."

She was a lovely woman and so like Mac. "His father left me when he was seven months old, so we were very close." She was looking at the pictures on the bright wall. "Then when he went to art school, I seemed to lose him. I'm remarrying next month and will be living in Edinburgh. Life must go on."

Marjorie stayed for a week.

Dolina was there every day. "I just can't wait to get the keys," she said, and sighed when Marjorie pointed out that you can't hurry the legal system.

When the signing was finally over, Lorna Jean broached the subject of Mac's possessions.

"They're yours," Marjorie said. "You meant a lot to him."

Lorna Jean wiped away a tear. "He helped me too." And she told Marjorie the story of the cancelled wedding.

Dolina couldn't wait to organize the shop, and the villagers approved of the way it was being updated.

"Och, between your cottage and the shop and the new house that's being built, this place is fairly looking up," Wee Maggie declared.

"We do our best." Her boss was smiling.

Not that Wee Maggie kowtowed to anyone. She had been snatched from a broken home and having made her way on the island, she could hold her own. She treated everyone from cleaners to directors of education, with equal disrespect. But her one virtue was that she was really good at her job.

"But you'll have to watch that wumman. Don't let her over the school door. She's quite capable of taking over."

"Well, you'd better watch your job. Some hours on the bus would suit her."

"That'll be the day."

Lorna Jean laughed as she went home, rushing past the shop and falling gratefully into the cottage where she took a sketch book from the box that Marjorie had told her to keep. There were two expensive real hair paintbrushes and a box of used artist's colours.

'I'll try the view,' she thought as she went out to the front steps. "Draw with your paintbrush," Mac had advised. The sky was fascinating. There never was a cloudless one in that part of Scotland; so mixing the colours, took a lot of careful observation.

Chapter 7

"Have you taken up art?" Dolina was patronizing, to put it mildly.

"Oh, I've always painted." Lorna Jean told the lie, remembering that a one-time boyfriend had once referred to her as 'a very convincing and artistic liar'.

"I've come to speak to you about Colin." She was pushing her way past the box and into the living room.

"Colin? Is something the matter?"

"Not really. He likes the school and should make a great difference to the results. No, it's just that the hours are not suitable. Once the shop gets underway, I'll need all the help he can give me, so I'd like him to work mornings at the school."

Lorna Jean's mouth shot open and she looked at this cheeky, interfering woman in blank amazement. There was a troubled silence. "Mrs McDonald, I am the person who decides how the timetable is made up. If your husband wants the mornings off, he'll have to give up the job. His post will be easy to fill. Do you want me to get in touch with the director of education?"

"Oh no, nothing like that, I just thought you wouldn't mind."

"Of course I mind. I won't be interfering in your business, so please leave me to mind my own. What does Colin think of it?"

Dolina's face flushed. "He doesn't know. Please don't mention it," and she marched off back to the shop where Colin was filling shelves.

The spell broken, Lorna Jean put the art box away, brewed up some tea, devoured six sandwiches — as anger always made her hungry — and, thus fortified, made her way to cry on Katrina's shoulder.

"The interfering bitch!" Katrina was furious. "I told you she would cause trouble. Mind you, that lily-livered husband of hers deserves all that's coming to him. But stand your ground. If the hours he works suit you, they'll just have to get someone in. My guess is that she never consulted him."

"Should I just ignore the whole thing?" Lorna Jean was twisting her hands.

"Leave it, but if she decides to go over your head, you can then point out that the timetable was made up to ensure the smooth running of the school and can't be changed. It calls for brandy and soda." Katrina was laughing and the strain fell from her friend's face. "You know I could fair fancy that Colin," Katrina confessed. "How come that a horror like that should end up with such a lovely man and here we are, two desirable girls, with not a man between us."

"It certainly makes you think," said her friend wistfully.

The long summer holidays loomed ahead. And Lorna Jean took to studying the situations vacant columns in the local papers to find herself a holiday job. What with buying the house and all the expense of moving in, the money would be useful and it would be a change of scenery.

Then she saw it — the real answer — children's entertainer at a holiday camp on the mainland. She phoned and, on the strength of her qualifications, arranged to interview the personnel manager on the following Saturday afternoon.

Katrina, when she heard of her plans, was really impressed. "I wish I was like you," she said. "You really are a go-getter."

"It's the only way to be. What's for you won't go past you, but you've got to rush out and grab before it passes."

They both fell about laughing.

The camp was on the Scottish south coast, noisy, cheerful and brash. It was, of course, the high season.

The personnel manager was one of nature's gentlemen, in

his well-tailored grey suit and old school tie, he was shaking her hand, hoping she had a comfortable journey down. "Actually, I'm very glad to see you. It's quite difficult to find someone who'll come for six weeks and, of course, that's the school holidays when we're at our peak for bookings."

Lorna Jean filled in the information asked for in the form and gave her banker, lawyer and the laird as willing to assure the head office that she was a person fit to be with young children.

"You don't look like a child molester," he laughed. "But with the five to ten age group, we've got to be careful. You will be with the children from nine till four. They'll dine with their parents at lunch time. You'll have a place in the dining room, the fourth seat at an allocated table. The children's supervisor will give you a time sheet. One day off per week and one evening. Chalet patrol while the parents are dancing or at the concert. What do you think?"

"I'd love it."

He stood up. "It's my coffee break. Would you like to join me?"

"Yes please."

They walked down the main path to the nicely decorated café where campers were enjoying soft drinks till the bars opened.

"The camp's only running half full at the moment," Stan Carter explained, as he brought coffee and delicious cakes.

A lovely blonde girl in a kilt, frilly white blouse and dark green jacket with the camp badge on the pocket came and joined them.

"If you get the job, Jean will be your boss." He laughed and introduced them. "And, of course, you'll be Auntie Lorna."

"My God, Auntie Lorna!" Katrina couldn't stop laughing when she was told. "And you'll be wearing the kilt. I don't believe it."

"And you should see the personnel officer who interviewed me."

Katrina shook her head. "And you'll be taking the

money," she said incredulously. "Some people do have jammy lives."

The letter confirming her appointment came the following Wednesday. The pay was unbelievable. The kilt wearing was compulsory.

Her mother was not happy. "It's not the type of thing I would approve of and those parents should be looking after their own children," she was grumbling.

Lorna Jean refused to be drawn into an argument. "Would you like a holiday in the cottage?" she asked.

"No thanks. It would be too much like work."

Her father, on the other hand, jumped at the chance. He was home on a long leave and was finally 'swallowing the anchor' as he put it. It was time for the shore work and he hoped to land a lecturing job at the Nautical College. "I'll come for the whole time" he said when he phoned next day with his piece of news. "It'll keep me out of your mother's hair and there's plenty I can do even to the garden. So, bless you my daughter."

There was the usual prize-giving, the staff lunch in the Oban hotel later, then it was back to the cottage to pick up the packed suitcase and leave the keys with Katrina.

"Mind you don't start making passes at him," Lorna Jean warned. "There's been enough scandal in the family already."

"With the bed and breakfast going at full tilt, I'll neither have the will nor the energy," she laughed as her friend staggered into the taxi with the suitcase on her way to the big adventure.

The personnel manager was at the main gate waving a smiling welcome. He took her suitcase and called up a commissionaire. "Chalet seventeen," he said. "I'll see you in the office at 9 a.m."

"What department are you in?" the commissionaire asked. The fellow must have been chosen for his appearance which was outstanding.

"Children's entertainment."

"Great! Your chalet mate is Vera, a great friend of mine. What's your name?"

"Just call me Auntie Lorna."

"Mine's Gus." He opened the door, threw in the case and went quickly up the chalet line.

"Hullo! I'm Vera. I'm hoping there'll only be the two of us, but you never know. Anyway, you can either have the single bed or the top bunk."

When Lorna Jean chose the single bed, Vera said "You're just in time for dinner. I suppose you can come with me to the staff canteen tonight until 'the little liver pill' gets you fixed up in the dining room."

Lorna Jean giggled at Stan's, the personnel manager's nickname.

"That's because he's Mr Carter and long ago his people made liver pills."

Vera was dressed in a smart suit and explained that as the camp announcer, she was not required to wear uniform. She also said that she was a white badge employee which allowed her access to the ballroom, coffee bars and the theatre. "I'm not the sporty type," she pointed out, "but if you are, there's a lot you can do in your spare time."

"Will I have a white badge?" Lorna Jean asked anxiously.

"Of course you will."

The staff canteen was set out for early dinner.

"I've got to get mine so that I can go back to my office to announce the campers' meals. It won't take long, so you can come with me. After that Jim, the other announcer, takes over."

The food was wonderful and watching Vera handle the announcement a novel experience.

The chalet door was open when they got back. Gus was reading a textbook seated on Vera's bunk bed. While on the bed, a handsome young man with riotous jet-black wavy hair was lost in a book of poetry.

"It's a good thing I trust him," Vera said indicating Gus. "He can get in here with his commissionaire's pass key."

"This is Callum, by the way. Great to know — he works in the kitchen!"

"Fancy a trip to the hotel?" Callum said. "All expenses paid. It's our evening off and Gus is having woman trouble."

Vera screamed with laughter. "The story of his life," she said to Lorna Jean.

He had a car in the car park, so they all piled in and regardless of speed limits, they sped up to the entrance and out onto the main coast road. Callum sang rugby songs and Gus joined in taking his hand off the wheel in a way that caused Lorna Jean to hold her breath.

The hotel was five star, set on a hill above the bay with a golf course in front and a sunset that looked painted on for extra effect. A flunky wearing a light brown suit with gold trimmings and a tall hat escorted them to a lounge where a piano was being played by a romantic musician. Gus tipped the flunky and they got armchairs from where Gus ordered coffee and biscuits.

"We're not waiting long," Callum said. "I'm on duty at six a.m."

Gus consulted his watch. "Just so as she's safely away on the last train," he said.

"What's all this in aid of?" Vera addressed Gus, her voice brittle.

"You tell them" he said to Callum as he poured coffee to hide his embarrassment.

"Well, at the beginning of last season, Gus got off with this English girl — just a holiday romance, you understand."

"So?" Vera's face was a study of expression.

"Well, after she went home, she started to pester him. When he ignored her letters, she appeared at his home. That caused trouble because he was back at college and his people thought there must be more to the romance. This morning, she came to the main gate to enquire if he was at the camp this season."

"But haven't you told her to jigger off?"

Lorna Jean was struggling to keep from laughing.

"I have, all the time. The security staff told her I wasn't on the camp and that I had a girlfriend called Vera."

The roar that Vera let out almost drowned out the piano music. "I'm not your girlfriend Gus. In fact, I'm nobody's girlfriend. In every generation of my family there has been one spinster and that's what I plan to be."

"My God." Lorna Jean started to laugh. "I've heard everything."

"Oh no you haven't," Callum said. "Come the end of the season, you'll know that Gus is the only fellow in the camp who gets his face slapped for doing nothing." He stood up and consulted his watch. "It's now after ten and the last train has gone. The camp is fully booked, so tomorrow you will be able to discharge your duties without hiding in the office or skulking in Vera's chalet."

"He really is a lovely lad," Lorna Jean said.

"Don't you start," Vera warned her as she went off to have a bath.

Chapter 8

The kilt and jacket had been collected from the storekeeper. She had signed on with the camp doctor as a temporary measure, and now she was on her way to Stan Carter's office to get her standing orders for the day.

'Great,' she thought. She was not on until the Punch and Judy show at 2 p.m. in the children's playroom, then on chalet patrol from 8 p.m. until 11 p.m.

The kilt felt heavy against her legs and the jacket was a bit too big, but with the frilly white lace of the blouse, it was not too bad.

When Vera, off duty for the afternoon, saw it, she screamed with laughter. "You look as if you should be doing the sword dance," she spluttered.

It was at dinner that Lorna Jean met her first campers, a lonely postmaster from Yorkshire and two trawlermen from Grimsby. Over the roast beef and Yorkshire pudding, the postmaster asked her out.

"I'd love to come with you, but I'm on duty from eight o'clock. You'll have plenty of partners when you go to the dance," she assured him.

She came out of reception with the list and was soon listening outside chalet doors for the sound of children crying. Three times she was standing in the wings of the theatre waiting for the compere to finish so that she could get calls for the parents to go to their crying children.

"What are you giving them to play with — razor blades?"

the theatre manager joked.

She was due a tea break so, having left everything all quiet, she went to the coffee bar. The sun, a ball of fire, was slowly sinking below the horizon, the sky was streaked with all the shades of scarlet and yellow. A band of happy campers hung over the rustic railing which faced the sea. "Isn't that a magnificent sunset," Lorna Jean said. Nobody answered.

Vera and Gus hailed her from a table. Callum appeared and bought her a coffee.

"I've decided to be your crying 'wean' escort."

"Oh great, we start in ten minutes."

By the time they reached 'H' line, Lorna Jean had mastered his life story. A three years' tour of duty with the RAF, then a university grant. "I intend to do honours," he said confidently. "What about you?"

"Nae hons," she laughed. "Even that was hard to come by. I'm teaching now."

"Teaching! What are you doing here?"

"It's a long story. I bought a house on a mortgage, so I thought instead of spending money on a holiday, I'd earn some money for a few weeks."

"You sound like my mother," he said. "She's always going on about money. Maybe it's because she's been twice a widow, the second time when I was nine."

They were coming up the steps to the main walkway when they heard a commotion coming from the open door of a lit-up chalet.

"I'd better check."

A girl was trying to get an unwilling small boy to bed and a toddler was staggering about the chalet floor.

"My dad's at home and my mum went away in the afternoon," the girl said.

"You stay there and I'll go up to security." Lorna Jean was so glad Callum was with her because there was something terribly wrong in this chalet. She checked the chalet list, but this number wasn't listed. "We'll find your mummy," she said reassuringly, and dug into her blazer pocket for the few sweets she had left.

The chief security officer came with Callum. "I'll leave it

to you people. I was on my way to get some sleep for tomorrow's five o'clock shift." The security officer took Callum's name. He was ex-CID and very suspicious. "They could be abandoned," he said stating the obvious. "But what to do with them?" His brain was the type that made no snap decisions.

"Why not take them to sickbay. There's a nurse on night duty and they have food and beds and safety."

"That's what we'll do," he said as if he had thought of the solution in the first place.

It took a week to solve the mystery when the father came to collect his family. He was away on a business trip and his wife had booked in with the children, left them and had gone off with her lover.

"I'm like that," Lorna Jean said. "Everything happens to me."

Next day it rained, so the playroom was full. Callum came to collect her and they took the local bus to the tiny fishing village with the one pub.

"It's a haven of peace," Lorna Jean said "and so romantic. I'd love to buy that old fisherman's cottage and retire there in my old age."

Callum laughed. "I'd prefer to travel," he said. "There's a great big world out there waiting to be explored."

They walked back to the camp hand in hand, refreshed and ready to deal with whatever the next day would bring in the form of drama and excitement.

The next few days were sunny, so it was sandcastle time and Lorna Jean started looking really healthy as all the cares of the previous year were wiped out. She also felt incredibly relaxed living her own life away from her mother's pessimistic view of things.

"It's Gus's birthday on Saturday, so we're having a party on the beach away from the camp. The boys are setting it up so keep your fingers crossed that the weather stays warm."

As the children were either coming or going on Saturdays, Vera and Lorna Jean had some time off during the day, so they volunteered to provide the paper cups and plates which they would buy in the nearby town.

"Let's skip lunch," Vera said "and buy a meal out."

They were in the camp uniform when they visited the quaint teashop which was famed for the best home-cooked snacks in the country.

"It's almost like celebrating your own birthday," Lorna Jean was sighing with pleasure.

"Better! We're not even a year older," Vera pointed out.

The woman who was sharing their small table, was leaning forward having noted their uniforms. "I see there's to be a great show at the camp theatre," she said. "Can anyone go or is it just for the inmates?"

Back at the camp, Lorna Jean collected her wages. She was a rich woman. Her school holiday pay was piling up in the bank and the camp pay provided the extras. She put the pay packet into her blazer pocket, changed into the soft wool sweater and tweed skirt, before going to join Vera on the beach.

The off-duty boys had built up piles of driftwood ready for the after-dark bonfire. Some of the band boys were fixing the canned music and Callum was staggering down the rocky path with a large cardboard box. "Will I be glad to get rid of this," he said. "The car's in for servicing and I'd to go to the home town to Gus's house to collect the cake his mother made. There's another one at home for the family tomorrow for when he goes home on his day off."

"Good heavens! Two birthday cakes." Lorna Jean was amazed. "My mother never even had one for me."

"Mine never even remembers my birthday," Callum said bitterly.

The flat rocks were being used as tables and people were bringing all sorts of goodies. There was a great feeling of goodwill and every girl that Gus had led down the chalet lines was there.

"Don't tell me he doesn't know about this?" Lorna Jean couldn't believe it.

"Dear old Gus is no detective. He was chosen on appearance — he looks good on the main gate."

Back on the camp, they could hear the strains of "Good Night Campers" from the ballroom.

The lads in charge of the bonfire set it alight. The music was turned on. Bottles were appearing all over the sand. The piper, straight from the ballroom, stepped into the doorway of a tumbled-down cottage which had been abandoned when the camp was built. Gus, just off duty, was being marched down the winding path. The piper struck up.

Out of the cottage rushed a partially-dressed pair of lovers. The revellers cheered. It was sheer magic. The cake was cut and the toasts disappeared in a flurry of sheer goodwill.

Lorna Jean, slightly tipsy, was in Callum's arms being fed birthday cake. Everyone had paired off and the night air was filled with romantic music. But it all fell apart when the police appeared.

"The real police," Callum said as he dragged Lorna Jean to her feet.

Gus, still in his uniform, stepped forward. "It's my birthday, sir." He was addressing the nearest policeman.

"Is it now!" The voice was grim. "That's no excuse for lighting that great fire without permission. It can be seen for miles up the coast."

"But I didn't light it." Gus was starting to sound like a five-year-old boy.

"I advise you all to get back to the camp. The controller will interview you in the morning."

Callum, stone cold-sober, saw Lorna Jean to the chalet. Vera was already there, sobbing softly under a mirror on which 'Happy Birthday' was written in soap.

Lorna Jean fell into bed and woke to Vera's voice on Tannoy. It was morning. "Will all entertainment department staff report to the office immediately after breakfast."

The little liver pill had his speech ready. It was all about thinking things out. Not undertaking outdoor parties and lighting bonfires without permission. He paused for breath and his eye caught the piper. "Put your machine under the table," he said. "It belongs to the firm and must be signed for. We can't have pipers playing indiscriminately," he said sternly.

Lorna Jean was on duty at the camp church. She kept the restless children at the back and distributed pan drops in the name of peace.

After the benediction, she made for the café to discuss the events of the previous night. "It's my turn," she said, and went to the counter.

Callum came to help.

Then she put her hand in her pocket for the money. It was not there. Then she felt the other pocket for her purse. It too had gone.

"Are you sure?" Callum looked startled.

"Could you pay and I'll go to security?" She was white faced with shock.

"What's your chalet number?" The security guard nodded his head. "That figures," he said. "Your chalet maid got in with the pass key when you were at the beach party. She's also made off with a lot of the campers' money. The police are on to it. If you're without money, Mr Carter will give you a sub!"

Lorna Jean felt terrible as she faced the personnel manager across the desk. "It was all I had," she groaned.

"People are always applying for subs," he assured her. "Would you like the full pay and we can take it from your next week's wages?"

"And to think she wrote 'Happy Birthday'." Vera just couldn't believe it. "She must have thought we were the ones having the party for my birthday. Mind you, she'd have bother getting her hands on my pay. It's round my waist in the body belt. If I go under a bus, don't bother to save the body — go for the body belt."

It was the first time Lorna Jean was able to laugh since the beach party. She was meeting Callum every evening and they were soon regarded as a pair.

Vera still regarded Gus as an older brother who used her to sort out his romantic problems. With Callum, Lorna Jean could relax. There was a solid feeling in their relationship and instinctively she knew he would never let her down. They had similar tastes like reading and travelling, and Lorna Jean got him interested in painting.

"I can't think we just have another week," he said as they lay, arms entwined, amidst the long coarse grass at the edge of the beach.

The campers were whooping it up, and in the distance they could hear Vera's voice on the Tannoy.

"I'll always remember this night," he said, his voice gentle and caressing. He wished there was not the responsibility of caring for his mother. They were very different people but he felt he had to finish his degree course.

Lorna Jean, on her part, was worried about the age gap. In the course of conversation she had discovered he was five years her junior.

On their last night, Vera had a small party. "I don't know how I'll get on in this chalet on my own," she said as they sat on the beds and talked.

Gus was leaving to go abroad. "He's a great athlete," Vera explained as he blushed and changed the subject.

"My head will be in a book," Callum assured them. His other friend, a medical student, had been working in the theatre.

"How did you manage to get that job?" Vera asked.

Duggie laughed. "When he interviewed me, the little liver pill asked if I'd any other experience beside being a student. I said I'd worked in the theatre at the Royal. Of course, I meant the hospital, but when he offered me the job, I just accepted it and loved every moment."

They all exchanged home addresses and drank a final toast to the future. Tomorrow morning they would resume normal life.

Chapter 9

Her father had the cottage shipshape and the garden was ablaze with late summer flowers.

Katrina invited them in for supper. There was a lot of news. "It's been a great summer for scandal," she said with relish. "Colin, the art teacher, has been seen with a girlfriend. And the swell who was building the luxury house, has gone bankrupt."

Her father sighed. "The Nautical College will be tame in contrast. And, of course, you know that Katrina's in love!"

"Never!"

"Yes, a new man called Tommy. He's working at the big house. I think it's the real thing this time."

"Oh!" suddenly Lorna Jean felt homesick for Callum. Everybody had somebody, but she had nothing. "I think I'll have an early night," Lorna Jean said to her father. "The farewell party at the camp was late and I've had all that travelling."

"Even with your tiredness you look a million times better," her father said gallantly as they left the coast clear for Katrina's new man and walked slowly up the winding road and past the art shop.

Lorna Jean was glad they were going home, for she expected a phone call from Callum.

"We're invited to Shona Campbell's party," her father said, but she told him to go alone and she ended up in bed with only a book for company.

The hustle of the next week with new registers to write, work sheets to prepare and four new five-year-olds to break in, took her mind off Callum. In her dreams she kept losing him and would wake up drenched in sweat and feeling awful.

On the Tuesday morning, there was a letter behind the door. "He's written," she murmured, then, on looking at the signature, found it was from Vera, with scraps of camp information which didn't mean a thing to her.

Dolina waylaid her on the way to the slipway where they were selling freshly caught fish. "If you can manage it when you're making up the new timetables, could Colin be off in the mornings."

Lorna Jean drew in her breath. "Colin" she said firmly, avoiding the eyes of the woman she hated, "will do the hours given. If that is not to your taste, then let him resign and leave the work for someone who can fit in with the rules."

She mentioned that to the laird when they met at the concert at Oban. "Do you think I'm being jealous and bitchy because she has a man and I haven't?" She asked the laird the question as they had a drink at the interval.

"Of course not," he assured her. "Your timetable is geared to use Colin at a time when you have your hands full with teaching the young children. Next time she broaches the subject, ask for an interview with the director of education. He'll soon send her packing."

The next day there was a phone call from the office. Lorna Jean was to go over after four o'clock.

"How are the island children?" Mr Wilson asked.

"They're doing well," Lorna Jean assured him, aware that this was not the real reason for the visit.

He lifted a letter from a parent and read out the contents regarding Mr McDonald's advances to her daughter. "Have you seen anything suspicious?"

"No! But then I'm not in the classroom with him."

"True. It is a worrying situation. How do you find him?"

"He tends to do his own thing — artwise, I mean. But his

exam results are very good," she said. "Funnily enough, I was considering asking for a talk with you because of his wife interfering with the running of his department. She keeps wanting him to have the time he comes to school altered to suit the art shop."

His face darkened. "If what has been alleged is true, maybe we should be sorry for her but, on the other hand, she must not be allowed to interfere with the running of the school. That's your job and I'm more than pleased with your efforts. Meanwhile, I'll have McDonald in and see what I can find out."

At that point, the secretary brought in coffee and biscuits.

"Now, tell me how you enjoyed your holidays. Where did you go, by the way?"

So Lorna Jean told him all about the camp.

"It sounds like a very interesting social experience." He was smiling and Lorna Jean felt that her problems with the school administration would soon be resolved. The director poured two more cups of coffee. "I think I have the solution to the problem. Mr McDonald's post is temporary on a twenty-four hour notice agreement. Last week, I got permission to appoint a full-time assistant for you. As it so happens, there is a very suitable applicant and he has art as part of his overall qualification. I suggest we keep Mr McDonald on meantime, but I'll send for him, show him the parent's letter and point out that any further complaints will result in instant dismissal. I will, of course, listen to his side of the accusation."

Lorna Jean left him to it. She felt sorry for Colin, but the matter was out of her hands. She wished she could talk it over with someone, but she had given a promise not to discuss the matter.

As it was, she bought herself a nice snack in the hotel and was glad to be back in the safe quietness of her own house.

It was the next evening that, on her way to Katrina's for tea and comfort, she saw Colin and a girl walk boldly into the shop which was closed for the day. 'That's not the girl whose mother complained,' she thought, but decided it could be innocent. 'Some extra tuition maybe? Besides, with Dolina there, not much could happen.'

Katrina had been to Oban in the morning and was very taken with the bedspread she had bought. "I met Dolina on the boat going over. Her mother's very ill so she was staying the night to give her sister a break. She's not my favourite person, but I did feel sorry for her and I can tell you that Colin will not be much help."

"You can say that again." Lorna Jean decided to change direction and led Katrina on to the subject of her new boyfriend which made the evening pass pleasantly.

"I think it's true love this time," Katrina said as she saw Lorna Jean to the door.

It was Wee Maggie who made the next move. "I need to have a slip to say that Anna McArthur is having extra art lessons from Mr McDonald and will not be on the bus at four o'clock," she said officiously.

"Leave it with me." She was in the art room before Wee Maggie could say more. "Will you take over here?"

"Sorry to be so fussy, but it's for the insurance," Wee Maggie said.

"I know that." Lorna Jean sighed.

"Can you come to my office at break time? It's very important. It's about Anna McArthur having extra art lessons."

Colin McDonald left the girl he was bending over. "I suppose so." His shifty eyes refused to meet her anxious look.

"What did he say?" Wee Maggie looked happy to be involved in a school scandal.

"Nothing!" Lorna Jean said. "I'll let you know before the four o'clock bell. Will you stay for a few more minutes, I've got to phone?" She went to the office, locked the door and phoned the director.

"I'll be over on the next boat," he said.

She went back to the classroom where Wee Maggie was happily enjoying the role of temporary teacher. She threw the sums cards on the desk. "No bad for a wumman who's never even been tae a teacher's college," she said to Lorna

Jean who was starting to be sorry she had.

The director appeared off the three o'clock boat, his expensively cut suit in sharp contrast to the casual wear of the other passengers.

Wee Maggie was back in the classroom to allow Lorna Jean to take Mr Wilson to her office.

"I gather that the girl whose mother complained is not the one who wants to stay for extra tuition?"

"That's right."

"And I take it you were not consulted?"

"No! The first I heard of it was from the bus attendant who came to me to ask if the girl's mother had given written permission."

"Which she hadn't?"

"No!"

There was a brief pause. "Could you take over the art class and send Mr McDonald to me?"

Lorna Jean's heart was thudding as she knocked on the door and entered the room. "I'll take over," she said. "Mr Wilson wants to see you in the office."

He hesitated and Lorna Jean lost her patience. "You'd better hurry. Miss Kerr has other duties and I can't stay here for long."

As she walked around the class, she was studying Anna McArthur who had turned into a hard-faced blonde. 'He's picked the wrong one this time,' Lorna Jean thought as Colin McDonald returned.

"He wants to see you," he said gruffly.

Terry Wilson looked shattered as he motioned her to sit down. "First of all, that girl must go home on the school bus. Will you see to that?"

"Certainly."

"I've suspended Mr McDonald on full pay. Without proof, there's nothing I can pin on him. I'll interview both mothers and I'll send a supply teacher to fill in." He smiled. "An elderly lady, you'll be relieved to hear."

Lorna Jean's head was thumping.

"It was one hell of a day" she confided to Katrina.

"But you handled it well," her friend said as she went home to toss for the whole of the sleepless night.

There was no known ending to the drama. Dolina's mother died and she sold the art shop to a bustling Englishman who made a great success of it. Colin disappeared, the replacement was appointed and although Wee Maggie kept trying to investigate, it always remained an island mystery.

Chapter 10

Lorna Jean couldn't believe it when Vera phoned. It was a voice from the past. "I want to ask you a favour. Would you be my bridesmaid?"

"You're marrying Gus?"

"You must be joking. No, I'm marrying my brother's friend, Allan Murdoch."

"You are! So there won't be a spinster in your generation of the family."

"No! Spinsters are out of date. By the way, Gus has been bitten by religion and is in love with a female Bible-puncher. It could even be love this time for him."

"Can we meet in Glasgow?"

"Yes, at the weekend. You can stay with my people for the weekend."

Vera had not changed. She was the caring cheerful person she always had been and Lorna Jean reckoned that Allan, when she was introduced to him, would make her friend a very good husband.

"The local banker, no less" Vera had confided when they were alone in the bedroom, examining the white lace wedding gown.."My mother made it and she has the material to make one for you." She brought out three bolts of lovely coloured shot silk.

"The dark green," Lorna Jean never hesitated, "and made in a simple design."

In the midst of it all, she was dying to ask if Vera had heard from Callum, but something held her back. Maybe he had someone else to love or was more interested in his career.

"I'm to be a bridesmaid," she informed Katrina. "That'll be my ploy for this year's summer holiday."

"Don't take on another one. You know the old Scottish saying, 'Three times a bridesmaid, never a bride.' I will be wanting you to be mine soon," Katrina pointed out.

"I'll remember." Lorna Jean forced a laugh she certainly did not feel. All this talk of love and marriage had left her with the empty feeling she thought she had conquered. But with the end of the school year approaching, she became too busy for brooding.

The older lady (actually in her late fifties) turned out to be a tower of strength and a kindred spirit. Mrs de Blec — 'Just call me Marlanda' — was a real Bohemian. "The 'Mrs' is a courtesy title," she confessed and kept Lorna Jean happy with tales of Paris studios, late-night revels, flights to tropical islands and visits to great houses and castles to paint portraits. She was, in addition, an inspired teacher who took the students with her and produced more work than Colin had managed in four times that time.

"How did you finally end up in Scotland?" Lorna Jean felt compelled to ask.

"One of your great clan leaders invited me to his castle to paint his daughter's portrait. No, I did not fall in love with him; I fell in love with your beautiful country. Now I am a landscape artist and have a studio in Edinburgh. When I saw the newspaper advertisement, I knew it was for me."

"God, isn't she something," Katrina marvelled as they watched her go down for the four-fifteen boat.

"Marlanda de Blec, a courtesy title no less. Why didn't I think of that?"

The school closed with the prize-giving and they all went for lunch in Oban.

As they parted, Marlanda gave Lorna Jean her card. "I feel that we shall meet again," she predicted.

It was all systems go for the wedding which was to be in Allan's village.

"That's Callum's mother's factory. She took over as manager when her husband died" Allan said as they went to his house for the show of presents. "She's coming to the wedding, so you'll meet her."

The empty feeling struck Lorna Jean again when there was no mention of Callum and she was too proud to ask.

"I've heard so much about you," Callum's mother said as she admired Lorna Jean's dark green dress. "The bride's dress was made from our lace," she explained "and that dark colour is a perfect foil."

The best man was the staidest male Lorna Jean had ever met and he danced as if an iron pole was fixed to his back.

The newly-weds left early in the evening.

"Where are you spending the holiday?" Vera asked as her bridesmaid helped her into the going-away outfit.

"Edinburgh" Lorna Jean said as she lifted her suitcase and threw the beige coat over the bridesmaid's dress. "I have a heavy date there," she said as she kissed the bride.

As soon as she could, she escaped. Dorothy was expecting her. Lorna Jean had also phoned Marlanda de Blec. "Oh do come," that lady had said. "I could well do with your help and your company."

Dorothy was so happy to see her. "You're looking so well and so organized," she said.

"How have you been?"

"Buzzing about as usual."

"When are you coming over to stay for a holiday in my little cottage?"

"As soon as the Festival is over. I'm counting the days."

Over late breakfast after the B & B guests had gone, Lorna Jean told Dorothy all about Marlanda.

"She's an awful woman. Actually, a real inspiration. She was really good to me when I was left on my own. I knew her through my son. He took private lessons from her although he was a different type of artist."

"She is a very good teacher," Lorna Jean said.

"Her life was tragic. She had Jewish blood and her father and mother were killed. She's always struck me as being very lonely." Dorothy was shaking her head.

"Aren't we all." Lorna Jean buttered a bread roll.

"Not really. I had my husband and you'll find there is someone for you. You're the marrying type."

It was almost as if she was getting some message over, Lorna Jean thought.

That evening she phoned Marlanda. It was so lovely to hear her fun-filled voice. "Come on over," she said and gave instructions about the easiest way to find her studio.

It had once been a meal mill — the water for turning the wheel was still there. It was the type of location suited to an artist but, somehow, in Lorna Jean's mind, it was not really Marlanda.

"What do you think of it?" she asked and it was really quite a hard question to answer.

"Mmm! It seems just right for the purpose."

"What purpose?"

"Well, hanging and selling pictures."

Marlanda's face clouded. "The trouble is I haven't sold any. That is why I applied for teaching to help with the expenses." She took Lorna Jean's hand, stroked it and the effect brought her out in goose pimples. This must have been what Dorothy was trying to tell her.

They had several drinks, and nuts and crisps were freely available.

"You will stay the night. We could be so happy in my lovely double bed."

Lorna Jean stood up and consulted her watch. "Sorry, I can't stay. I'm meeting an old boyfriend for dinner." She had thought up the excuse on the spur of the moment and had trouble controlling the tremor in her voice.

"That's a pity. But do come again before you leave Edinburgh. I'd like you to consider becoming my partner in business."

"It was a dreadful experience," Lorna Jean said as she related the events of the evening to Dorothy.

"I should really have explained things better. But I honestly never thought she'd approach you. They usually sense if a woman is their type."

Dorothy sighed — "This world would be less complicated if only sex was straight forward. Let's have a good old hot chocolate before we go off to our single beds. And you'd better pray to be forgiven for all the lies you've told to that poor woman."

Chapter 11

After the adventures of the Edinburgh trip, Lorna Jean was glad to be back on the island and all set for the new school year. A lot of improvements had been made and the classrooms extended to cope with the growing number of pupils.

Tony McIntosh, who had been appointed her deputy, was a young, married man with three children. They would be enrolled in a Oban school. "I really would hate to teach my own offspring," he laughed. His wife taught infants part-time and they lived on the mainland.

Wee Maggie — "Miss Kerr but no fur much longer," she explained as she flashed an engagement ring.

"Does that mean we'll be losing you?" Lorna Jean's heart sank.

"Oh no. I'll be marrying the odd-jobman at the Estate. We'll be renting a cottage and I'll keep on working. No fear of unwanted pregnancy at my age." She was laughing, bubbling over with pure joy which made her boss feel like the last spinster in captivity.

Katrina was depressed — an unusual state of mind for her. Her boyfriend had gone to work in Liverpool.

"Well, you'll just have to go there with him," Lorna Jean said as she prepared the supper of cheese pie.

"You are joking. Have you see that place? I'd die from lack of air."

"Not if you really loved him. Love conquers all."

Katrina, eating obviously for comfort, sighed and said, "I would not confess this to any other living soul, but he didn't ask me to go and he hasn't been in touch."

Lorna Jean refilled her friend's cup but refused to offer any advice. Having been in the situation herself, she knew how only the people involved were able to act and secretly felt that Katrina was better the way things were.

The school was running smoothly and the numbers of pupils kept rising as new houses were built and young families moved in.

Wee Maggie had fixed her wedding date. The ceremony was to be in the church; the reception in the school hall, to which all were invited. Her groom had been in the Navy and he was wearing his dress uniform. The bride wore a white suit with a silver thread woven in, which looked really dignified. "The long skirt will hide my rickets" she joked. Poor Maggie's bad legs were a legacy from her undernourished childhood.

Lorna Jean gave her the headdress she'd worn at Vera's wedding and the shoes that were alright for a wedding but no use for tramping the island roads. Katrina bought the flowers and the laird laid on the buffet.

"I'll do the same for you," he promised Lorna Jean.

"It's almost as good as planning your own wedding," Katrina said and wondered why her friend failed to answer.

It was the best day the island had seen. Half-term holiday and they all gathered in the church. The groom was so enthusiastic that he said "I do" before the minister asked. The reception was wonderful, and the honeymoon spent in the new cottage was everything Wee Maggie had always dreamed of, and the next day she would be back on the bus, coping with the high spirits of children who had been released after a hard day's work at school.

"My, but it was a great day." 'Mrs' was the title that Wee Maggie would have loved but even with the glamour of the wedding, to the pupils she was still the bus lady and a target for teasing.

"They aw have it far too easy," she told Lorna Jean. "At their age, I was washing the orphanage floors."

Chapter 12

There had never been a sports day on the island and Tony McIntosh expressed surprise.

"You have my permission to organize one so long as I'm not compelled to join in." It was all Lorna Jean would have needed, she thought, as she did her best to keep ahead with the bookwork.

So the 12th of May was set aside and she took a small sum from the school funds to provide prizes.

"It'll be the wettest day in the year, just you wait and see," Wee Maggie predicted.

But May on the islands is a lovely time. The air is so clear and the summer mists which obscure the view were still to come, as was the autumn rain. The day dawned with the pink sunrise rising in the east. The laird had given his workers the day off on full pay; so there was plenty of outside support. The small admission fee was a good boost for the school funds and several women set up stalls.

Lorna Jean forgot about the paperwork and went so far as to win the adult egg and spoon race. She even dug her heels in at the tug of war. There was a display of gymnastics by the older boys who had been trained by the visiting PE teacher. Everyone voted it one of the best days on the island and there was a feeling of friendship that had replaced the old clannish atmosphere which had formerly been the way of life.

"Would you like to join the Art Circle?" Tony McIntosh asked. "It's pretty informal. We meet once a month and bring our pictures. Twice a year we have an exhibition."

"I'm not all that good," Lorna Jean confessed, but she was really interested.

"The best way to learn is by being with like-minded people. My wife had never handled a palette knife before she met me. Now she's the one who makes the pin money with her art. The other advantage is that you can get the material at cost price."

"You've sold me the idea." The monthly trip to the mainland, meeting new people and maybe even having a picture hung, was very appealing.

The first meeting was a shock to the system — portrait painting. The lecturer from Glasgow Art School had them making the likeness of an old man with such an interesting face, that he must have had a life that could have made a best-selling story.

Lorna Jean enjoyed following the lecturer's instructions and although her effort was basic to say the least, she felt that another avenue had opened. She spent the next month capturing her friends' likenesses and was really hooked on the new hobby.

Her real talent lay in landscape painting and she loved it when one of the top painters in this field gave the monthly lecture. "You have a real flair for colour," he told her and it made her day.

She decided that for the summer exhibition she would do the view from the cottage. Nor was she deterred when Katrina caught her painting the masterpiece in the shadow of her front door. That, of course, was one of the advantages of the enterprise. It could be lifted and laid according to circumstances.

She screwed the tops on the tubes of oil paint, threw the brushes into a jar of turps and, while what she had already painted dried in the cool sea breeze, she was ready for any morsel of village news that her friend was willing to exchange for creamy coffee and doughnuts.

Katrina, as usual, came straight to the point. "Wee Maggie's pregnant!"

"You're joking."

"No, she was seen coming out of the antenatal clinic yesterday."

"But that doesn't necessarily mean that she's starting a family. She could even have been helping out, after all she does have quite a lot of spare time morning and afternoon."

"Well, time will tell. She'll have to tell you."

"I suppose so. She is, after all, married." Lorna Jean wondered where all this was leading to.

Katrina dunked the doughnut in the coffee and looked her friend in the face. "Do you mind if I apply for her job?"

"It won't be for me to decide. You have to write to the office. Ask for your name to be put on the list for any vacancy that comes up. They probably have other people but, to be fair, everyone gets a chance to be interviewed. Write tonight and they'll get it tomorrow."

"I'd love that job," Katrina said wistfully.

Next day, Wee Maggie took Lorna Jean aside. "I haven't been feeling too good," she said, "so I went to the doctor — I'm pregnant."

"Great!"

"You don't think I'm too old?"

"Of course not. How's the happy father?"

"Over the moon. He hasn't to think about his job or can we afford all this. He's going round offering drinks already. Will I have to resign?"

"You can go until your maternity leave, after that it's up to you."

"Oh, I'm so glad I spoke to you. I wanted you to be the first to know," Wee Maggie said, leaving Lorna Jean feeling very guilty indeed.

When Katrina came over in the evening, she said she had posted the letter. "Keep your fingers crossed," she said.

"For what?" Lorna Jean asked. "Wee Maggie is indeed pregnant, but she's taking maternity leave and keeping on the job."

"But she can't work with a new baby."

"She's having someone look after it — there's a job for you."

"No thanks!" Katrina sounded sulky, but stayed for supper

just the same and, as the evening wore on, became more like her old self. It did not require a career psychologist to decide that handling children was not for her.

"I met a nice fellow in the bar in Oban when I went over to post the letter in the general post office," she said. "He works for the Forestry Commission."

"That's good."

"Yes, we're going to the concert on Saturday night. That's more exciting than having your head done in by a bus load of screaming weans."

"I think you could be right. It seemed like a good idea at the time." Katrina agreed.

The following Tuesday she came over just as Lorna Jean was finishing the landscape. "It just has to be varnished and framed," she explained as she took it off the easel.

"It looks very professional." Katrina dismissed the art treasure and took out a buff envelope from which she drew a large form from the Education Department.

"Do you want help to fill it in?"

"You must be joking. The money is peanuts and the questions are insulting — things like marital details. Have you a criminal record? Can you provide two referees?" She tore the form into small pieces. "Victor says to have nothing to do with it."

"Who is Victor?"

"The fellow from the forestry. He was over last night. Had great ideas about what I could do with the house. Quite inspiring."

"I think that's the best thing for you."

"Are you sure you don't mind?"

"Not me. I think you are cut out for something more glamorous," Lorna Jean said, and meant it. In fact, a niggling thought kept recurring. 'Get out of teaching before you reach forty,' a school friend had warned her years ago. 'Once you get entrenched, it's difficult to let go and it destroys your personality.'

'A freelance artist,' she thought as she prepared her picture for hanging at the Art Club Exhibition. 'That's it.' She had offered her services for the Saturday morning showing and had a great time interviewing all sorts of tourists who were serious in their desire to buy a reminder of their happy holiday. She had noticed a well-dressed business gent examining her own picture in great detail. Eventually he made the decision and came over with the catalogue in his hand. "I'd like to buy that picture." He was pointing to Lorna Jean's, the one she had painted from her doorstep. "Would you tell me how to contact the artist."

The artist laughed. "You're talking to her," she chuckled. "If you want to take it now, I'll wrap it for you, or would you like to leave it with a red spot on? I have another picture I can use to fill that space."

"I'll take it now," he said and whipped out his cheque book.

As she went to wrap the picture, he took another look. "Great!" he said. "That frame exactly matches my furniture."

She was, if the truth be told, sorry to see the picture go, but a cheque for £60 was quite something for a first-time artist. At the end of the show when people were taking really good pictures home because nobody had bought them, she felt that this must be beginner's luck in her case and maybe a freelance artist might not be the alternative for her after all. And this decision was reinforced by the fact that her second picture had been rejected.

Chapter 13

Vera phoned as Lorna Jean was about to spend an evening tidying the garden. "We just arrived in Oban," she explained. "Tomorrow we're sailing to Iona. What about having dinner with us at the hotel?"

"I'd love that," she said as she kicked off the gardening shoes and went to dress in time for the six-thirty boat.

"Look at that tan," Vera said as she came down the stairs to meet her friend. "Let's have a plate of sandwiches and a pot of coffee to sustain us until dinner at eight-thirty. Allan's at a conference and won't be back until after eight. It's so great to see you again. In fact, only last week we had Callum and his fiancée drop in to see us and bring a belated wedding present."

Lorna Jean felt her heart sink as Vera, unaware of the situation, rattled on.

"What he sees in that woman, I'll never know. She's bossy, rude and old enough to be his mother." And then, without pausing in her helter-skelter conversation, she said, "And what about you?"

"Oh, doing well enough to have bought the cottage on a mortgage and the school numbers are up; so I'm due more money."

"What's the social life like?"

"Great — it's almost as good as the camp."

"Yes, those were the days. Although I'm happily married, I miss the company. Allan is the original workaholic; and there's not much going on around the neighbourhood," Vera sighed. "At least, you're fancy-free, so enjoy it while you can."

Vera wasn't really cut out to be a banker's wife, Lorna Jean reckoned, and was stopped in her summing up of her friend's situation by the return of Allan who looked grey and tired and not really all that pleased to be sharing his wife with her friend at dinner.

She suddenly made the decision. "I really have to go," she said. "The boat leaves at eight-forty." She did not add that the last one was at ten.

Vera jumped up and said "Sorry you can't wait for dinner, but thanks for coming. That was a lovely evening and I enjoyed the break."

"Have a good time in Iona."

Allan's handshake was like a limp lettuce and his face expressed a certain horror at 'good time' being used in connection with Iona. "It will be a spiritual experience." His tone was reverent and disapproving.

As Lorna Jean kissed her friend, she noticed the tears were starting to run down her cheeks. "Cheerio!" she said as she lifted her handbag. "Now that you know where I am, keep in touch." Allan was already on his way to the dining room.

"It was a terrible evening and the husband was so unfriendly," Lorna Jean said as she sipped a brandy and soda in Katrina's friendly sitting room.

"Men get very jealous of the friends their wives had before marriage," Katrina said after hearing the story. "They all take the 'forsaking all others' a bit too seriously."

"I hadn't known that."

"Oh yes, it can cause a lot of ill will."

"Funny," Lorna Jean said, "I hadn't thought of it that way. Vera and I were just workmates. She was friendly with someone else at that time. So was I, as a matter of fact, and the other depressing thing was she told me that he had visited her and brought his girlfriend."

"It certainly was not your evening." Katrina was topping up the glass, being sympathetic, and her very presence helped her friend.

"Maybe it's better not to look back," Lorna Jean decided.

"I never do — much too busy with the present," Katrina said.

Back in the cottage as Lorna Jean prepared for bed, she felt sorry for Vera who had been so bubbly, but was now being held back by her grey-suited husband.

As she lay listening to the waves lapping on the shore, she felt happy with things as they were — until the right fellow comes along, she reckoned as she went slowly to sleep.

Chapter 14

Katrina was having the house extended and was announcing her engagement to Victor, who was packing-in the forestry and, when they were married, would be her partner in the small hotel that was so badly needed on the island.

Planning permission was fraught with difficulty. "If I see another architect, official planner, or loony lawyer, so help me I'll commit hari-kari," she groaned.

"It'll get you nowhere," Lorna Jean warned her. "Just keep calm as you keep telling me to do and all will be well."

"To change the subject" Katrina said, "Victor thinks we should nip over to the Oban Registry Office one fine Saturday and tie the knot. He's very conventional. Wouldn't even share the caravan we'll have to doss down in while the hotel takes shape."

"He sounds like a really nice man. Have you fixed a date?"

"As soon as legally possible. Would you be a witness?"

"Oh yes, and the great thing is this will be my second time, so I can refuse all other requests by pointing out the 'three times a bridesmaid, never a bride' rule."

"If you like bright red hair and a long beard to match, you'll love the best man. His name is Hamish and he writes poetry." Katrina was laughing. Then she sobered. "I know this sounds ridiculous," she said "but could you keep this a secret. I've been let down so often that I won't believe it until I have the ring safely on the finger and the certificate in my handbag."

"Of course I will," Lorna Jean promised. "After all, I know

the feeling."

A week later, Katrina invited Lorna Jean to Oban. The banns were going up and she had to meet Hamish before the wedding.
"It's on a Saturday to save anyone having a day off work," Katrina explained.
They were to meet outside the registry office and Lorna Jean spotted Hamish immediately — the hair was russet and the beard matched. He was handsome in a rugged sort of way, and a good-natured smile revealed fine white teeth as he stepped forward to greet the couple.
"So this is Lorna Jean." The voice was lilting and the handshake was firm.
"So what now?" Katrina asked.
"Well, before we go any further, could you both come to the jeweller's where four clocks have been set aside. In case you don't know, this is the traditional gift from the best man to the happy couple, and you'll choose the one you like." Hamish put his arm through Lorna Jean's and they all set out down the main street.
It didn't take long and soon they were in the hotel where they drank a toast before going back to Lorna Jean's cottage to deposit the clock and the bridesmaid's gift of a fine picture commissioned to specification by Katrina and painted by a well-known professional artist. She had actually wanted her friend to do this, but Lorna Jean said she deserved something better. "It's terrific. Just what we wanted," they said as they made the final plans for the wedding.

The chosen Saturday was brilliant.
"Happy the bride the sun shines on," Lorna Jean whispered as they sat on the boat, well away from the other passengers. The floral buttonhole flowers were hidden in their handbags. The bride wore an off-white suit; the bridesmaid a dark green dress. They had hired a room at the hotel for the girls. The men, who were in another hotel, joined them at the registry office and, in no time, they were having a celebration lunch before the happy couple caught the train for Glasgow.

"It's a great way to tie the knot," Hamish said as they walked back to the hotel. "It saves so much ill will and everybody getting so stressed."

"Don't I know." Lorna Jean sighed and told Hamish the whole sad story of her aborted wedding . . . . .

"That was dreadful." He topped up her glass and there was genuine concern in his voice. "Do you still feel bitter?"

"Not really. I'd had a feeling something was wrong, but felt I had to go through with it for the sake of both our families. When he actually phoned to say it was off, I felt great relief. He had, of course, made another girl pregnant. It was hard to take, but I changed my job and bought the cottage on a mortgage."

"Good for you. I should really thank that horror of a man. If all that had not happened, I'd never have met you."

"You fairly impressed Hamish," Katrina said as they drank coffee in the caravan. "He hasn't stopped talking about you since the wedding."

"He's nice."

"Yes, and going places. He's just graduated with a PhD."

"Never!" said Lorna Jean. "I thought he worked in the forestry."

"No, that's just until he gets a post to suit his qualifications. His father is very wealthy but believes in letting his sons make their own way in life. He's the eldest of four boys."

Work had started at the hotel and they were making great headway.

"Hamish has a week off and is coming over to help Victor. You'll have to come to the caravan every evening to keep the gossips from accusing me of having it off with two men," Katrina was explaining.

Lorna Jean laughed. "If they're talking about you, they'll be leaving the rest of us alone," she chuckled. Then the thought struck her. "Why don't you all come over to me for tea!"

"Oh, that would be terrific. I'll fill up your fridge because you have no conception of how much food that pair can shift," Katrina said. "And besides, I can use the extra time to give them a hand. The local lads have been really wonderful and we're actually ahead of time."

It was one of the best weeks in Lorna Jean's life. They were a foursome in complete harmony, and the cottage took on a real lived-in atmosphere.

"I don't want to go back to the forestry," Hamish said.

"Well don't." It was a typical remark from Katrina who always lived for the moment.

Hamish looked shocked. "I'd have to give them notice. My appointment as lecturer in Edinburgh University is not until October."

'Good for you,' Lorna Jean thought and was glad that Hamish was so reliable and dedicated to duty.

Chapter 15

The hotel was officially opened, and Hamish had gone back to the forestry job. Lorna Jean was teaching by day, and Katrina and Victor were tied up with running the hotel, which had just been granted a licence.

Wee Maggie, who had been too heavily pregnant to keep on coping with wild pupils and unmade roads, had finally given notice of her retiral. Only Lorna Jean knew that twins were expected. "Don't tell anyone," Wee Maggie warned.

The news was official when Wee Maggie was airlifted off the island. Lorna Jean went to visit her in the maternity wing of the mainland hospital. As the nurse brought in the healthy boy and girl, Wee Maggie introduced them to Lorna Jean.

"What a turn out for a woman who had decided to be an old maid," she chuckled.

"Who's running the bus?" she asked.

"A girl called Shona who never laughs."

Wee Maggie seemed pleased. "She'll never last," she said, looking to the future when the twins were at school and the bus would be without an attendant.

It happened sooner than she thought. Just at the end of her maternity leave, the young girl gave in her notice.

"They offered to keep me on," she told Lorna Jean "but I just couldn't keep control."

"You were too near their own age to have authority over them."

When she was marking examination papers, the phone rang. It was Maggie.

"The office was asking if I would be back at the end of the maternity leave."

"So?"

"My mother-in-law was visiting and has offered to look after the twins. She just dotes on them. Just as I never thought I'd ever be a mother, she never thought she'd be a grandmother. She lives alone on the mainland, so she'll move into our spare room and let out her house."

"That's worked in very well," Lorna Jean said and felt melancholy. 'Everybody is having happy endings but me,' she thought as she returned to the marking.

There had been no phone call, letter or postcard from Hamish.

"He'll just turn up one day," Katrina assured her, too busy with her new life to spare a thought for her friend.

When Maggie came over one evening, it was to ask her to be godmother at the christening of Jane and Rory. "We'll have a breakfast in the hotel afterwards. Katrina is giving me a good discount."

"Will you buy two sets of silver baby scissors in gift boxes," Katrina asked when she heard Lorna Jean was going to the jeweller's to get a silver bangle for Jane and a porridge spoon for Rory.

The three clocks that had been on show were still unsold when she revisited the jeweller's. In a mad moment, she asked to see the one that Katrina had rejected and Hamish had liked. It cost all of a month's salary but worth every last cent.

"Let's set up a baby shower," Katrina suggested. "Free tea and biscuits and leave a small gift for the twins. I'll set up a table in the corner, dress it up with blue and white streamers, and put our gifts on to start it off. The island ladies would do anything for tea and a blether. After the christening would be a great time. Sunday afternoon is a good idea when everyone is bored."

Lorna Jean painted a poster and they attached it to the hotel's front gate. 'Baby shower' would be explained to a few people and the news would be carried round the island like the fiery cross of the old days.

Wee Maggie was doubtful. "I'm not all that popular," she sighed. "Maybe nobody will turn up."

"Oh, I wouldn't say that," Katrina assured her. "We already have gifts in the shower."

Lorna Jean helped by mentioning the event to any of the mothers who came to collect their children who did not travel by bus. She also offered to help with the serving of the tea and biscuits. Wee Maggie was there to offer thanks for the mindings and it was a great afternoon.

"We must have more gatherings like this," Katrina said. "This hotel is just right for a meeting place."

When the ladies had all departed and Victor had taken Wee Maggie and her shower of gifts home in the car, the two friends put their feet up, drank coffee and exchanged gossip.

She had her back to the door and hadn't seen him come in, and it was only when a pair of hands came over her eyes and the lovely voice said "Guess who!" that Lorna Jean knew Hamish had come back into her life.

"This calls for more than coffee," Katrina said, but Hamish said he would prefer coffee, a choice echoed by Victor when he appeared.

"See what the wind blew in." Katrina was topping up the coffee, offering sausage rolls and home-baked cake.

Hamish reached for a ham sandwich. "I thought I'd come over to see you all before I go over to Edinburgh," Hamish explained and Lorna Jean felt a stab of disappointment that he had not made the journey specially to see her.

"All the forestry boys were asking for you," Hamish said. "We must have a reunion."

As the man-talk went on, Lorna Jean and Katrina went to help in the kitchen.

"I'll have to go. There's a whole pile of marking to do before tomorrow." And before Katrina could do anything about it, her friend was well on the way home.

"Where is she?" Hamish asked when he came back into the room.

"Back home to mark school papers." She was clearing up as she asked "Are you staying tonight?"

Hamish's face looked stricken. "There doesn't seem much point."

Victor laughed. "You know the old saying about faint heart . . ." he said.

Katrina shook her head. "Listen to who's talking. I can tell you here and now that if I had not done the proposing, neither of you would be sitting here this evening."

Hamish looked flushed. "You see, I brought a small present for Lorna Jean."

"Well," said Victor, "my advice is — get the hell over there before she gets the head in the papers. We'll keep your room."

"Good," said Hamish.

"My God," said Katrina.

Chapter 16

The tears splashed down Lorna Jean's flushed cheeks as she stumbled along the dark road with the wind from the sea lifting her hair and sending the waves crashing on the shore. As she approached the cottage, she fumbled in the pocket of her dark green coat and found the keys.

The fire was still warm, so she banked it up, lit all the lamps and was just about to finish the few papers she had to mark, when the door bell rang.

"It's Hamish."

Her heart leapt up as she undid the chain and, before she could protest, was in his arms.

"I've brought you a present."

Lorna Jean stepped back and took the small artistically wrapped jeweller's box that he had taken from his inside pocket. The small enamel brooch in the shape of a butterfly was in such good taste.

"It's lovely," she stuttered as they entered the cosy room and sat side by side on the sofa. "Sorry I had to rush off, but I've got to mark that lot of papers for first thing tomorrow."

"Yes, Victor told me."

There was an embarrassed silence.

"Tell you what," Lorna Jean said. "You make the supper and I'll rattle them off."

"That's a good idea." The strained look had left his face and soon he was singing in the kitchen, rattling the utensils and thoroughly enjoying himself, while Lorna Jean tore through the marking.

"I've really missed you." He was dishing up the sausage and mash as if he'd been a kitchen chef all his life.

"You're a handy man to have around!" Lorna Jean was stuffing the corrected papers into her briefcase and looking approvingly at his efforts.

"You get plenty of practise if you're one of a large family. By the way, would you like to meet them?"

"If they're all as nice as you — yes."

"Nobody is as nice as me," he said and gave her a smacker of a kiss.

Three weeks later, his mother phoned to invite her for the weekend. "I'm really looking forward to the meeting. Hamish never stops talking about you."

Lorna Jean was engulfed in self-doubt. What if it all went wrong? What if he changed his mind? His family might not approve of her and there were her father and mother.

On the Friday night, she hardly shut an eye and, on Saturday as she dressed, she hated what she saw in the mirror. "I'm not ready for this," she told herself.

She was wearing a dove-grey suit and a jade green blouse with the brooch Hamish had brought, at the neck. I could be ill, she thought, too ill to travel — then the bell rang. It was no use. Hamish was on the doorstep.

"You must have started out early."

"The middle of the night."

She laughed.

"Even the dog was still snoring," he said as she lifted the expensive flowers from the kitchen sink and wrapped them in the florist's paper.

"For your mother," she explained.

"She'll love that. We live in a flat which is great but she misses the garden."

He thought she was tired on the way up the motorway. It was not like her to be so quiet. But Lorna Jean was having a panic attack. 'I'm not ready for this,' she thought as she fought the impulse to cancel the visit. 'But it is only a social visit. Nobody is forcing you to do anything,' she told herself.

"We'll have to leave the car in Rory, my brother's garage, and walk the rest as there is no parking." He had driven off the motorway and they were approaching a neat bungalow.

As they approached, a tall, dark-haired man was swinging open the wide gate to let the car in. "You must be Lorna Jean." He shook her hand and his smile was so like that of Hamish that she felt reassured. "Shona is floor-walking with David. He's teething. We've been up all night."

"Let that be a lesson to you," David's mother said. "Here am I, married to a doctor and he can't even cure teething troubles."

They left after a glass of champagne for everybody, except Hamish, who had to make do with Coke. "I'm driving later," he explained.

"Good God man, surely you can stay overnight. There's plenty of room in the flat."

"True, but Lorna Jean has to teach at school tomorrow."

"Tell Mum I'll be over tomorrow."

Shona was draping David over her shoulder as they left.

"She's a beautiful girl," Lorna Jean said as they set out to walk to the parents' flat.

"Not as pretty as you are." Hamish was holding her hand and somehow it felt just right.

The flat door was open when they walked up the two flights of stairs, and the mother, a little roly-poly figure with white hair piled high on her head, stood smiling on the threshold. "Come on in," she said and Hamish hugged her.

"Meet Lorna Jean," he said and the kiss restored her confidence.

In the bedroom as she took off her coat, the mother said, "I'm so pleased to meet you. Hamish keeps telling me about you."

The father was in a wheelchair in the large, airy room that commanded a wide view of Princes Street.

"Isn't this marvellous," Lorna Jean said after they shook hands. She wondered what had made him disabled. Sitting in the chair, he looked so like Hamish. The same features, the hair colour, the broad shoulders.

"It's a great flat," he said. "A window on the world. And

at the back, there's a lift so we can get out to all the clubs."

The mother had joined them. "You can have lunch any time," she said.

"Right now!"

"He takes a lot of filling, be warned." She patted Lorna Jean's arm as she led her to the dining room.

It was a beautifully cooked meal and the mother gratefully accepted Lorna Jean's offer of help with the washing-up. "Hamish will see to his father," she said as she ran the hot water and soon the soapy suds were ready for the wash-up.

Lorna Jean felt so much better, as she dried the plates and put the cutlery in the spoon drawer.

"You must come again to meet Donny, my youngest," the mother said.

"It must have been hard work with four boys," she said.

"Not really, Father had plenty of money for domestic help and the boys did their bit — still do — and I have my helpers. Donny is at university and Ian is in the Army, so they're all doing well."

Lorna Jean was dying to ask what had happened to her husband, but she didn't have the courage.

The kitchen restored, they went back to the splendid sitting room.

"We'll soon have to be getting back," Hamish said looking at his watch after his mother had brought out the last photograph album. "It's a long haul and we both have livings to earn."

"I've really enjoyed my visit."

"You'll come again?" There was something about his mother's eagerness that made her wonder about the past life of Hamish.

"Of course I will," she said, hoping that all would be well.

"What happened to your father?" she asked. He had looked so handsome and healthy in the album pictures.

The car swerved slightly and his face clouded. "Six years ago, I was playing in a rugby tournament and he was driving to the Borders to spectate, when a drunk driver lost control, and there was a three-way crash. Among his other injuries, he suffered a fractured spine which can never be repaired."

"I'm sorry."

"He has taken up the threads of his life again, but he took his frustration out on me for so long that I was forced to leave home. He had this obsession that had he not have been forced to go to this rugby match by the family, who thought he should be there to support me, all this would never have happened."

"But it was all in the hands of fate."

"I know, but try telling him that."

They drove on in silence. Lorna Jean had to suppress the impulse to cradle him in her arms. He had suffered a loneliness that she could relate to.

"Are you staying overnight with Katrina and Victor?" she asked.

"Yes."

He was at the door of the cottage very early. Not too early, for Lorna Jean who liked to leave everything tidy, before she left.

"I'll walk you to the school," he said as she rushed around.

"That'll cause talk," she giggled as he swept her into his arms.

They left each other at the school gate as the bus drove in, the children staring out of the windows.

"I'll be in touch," he said and disappeared.

Chapter 17

"Why don't you phone him?" Katrina was folding paper napkins and listening to Lorna Jean who had arrived in a distressed state.

It was almost four months since the visit to his parents and nobody had heard from him.

Victor came in with a box of supplies. "He's always been like that — very casual and laid back," he assured them. "I think his father's accident upset him and changed his attitude to life. My advice is to leave well alone. He'll come when he's ready."

'So it was to be another lonely Saturday night,' she thought — self-pity bearing down on her like a black cloud.

She was painting the background for the floral picture she had planned, when the door bell rang.

"Hamish." She rushed into his arms.

"Can I come in?" His voice sounded flat and tired and his feet dragged as he came into the kitchen.

"I'll put the kettle on — is something wrong?"

He sat down, put his head in his hands and said "My father died."

"Died!" Lorna Jean was unable to find words, so she cradled him in her arms.

The kettle whistled insistently, so she rushed to put it off and infused the tea. He had regained his self-control by that time.

"Maybe it was all for the best," she said as she cut up

sandwiches and sliced a newly-baked gingerbread.

"I suppose so. He died in his sleep and what hurt me most was that I got cut out of his will."

"But maybe he just thought the others needed the money more," Lorna Jean said reasonably.

A dark, angry look came into his face. "That was just him getting at me from the grave."

Lorna Jean did not wish to hear more, so she changed the subject. "Would you like to stay here for the night?" she asked. "You can have my bed and I'll camp out on the sofa. Katrina is running a silver wedding tonight. We could see them at church tomorrow!"

"Are you sure that's alright? I don't want to spoil your weekend."

Lorna Jean giggled. "There's no handsome prince coming to take me to the ball, so I had decided to paint a picture and watch my favourite programmes on the television, like the good virgin that I am."

"I'll join you," he said.

"This is great," she said as she nestled in his arms. It felt so right.

Next morning at church time, they set out to meet Katrina and Victor.

"Ah ha! and what will the pupils think."

"Shut up."

Katrina with her underlying sixth sense knew something was wrong.

"Hamish came to tell me his father had died."

"I'm so sorry."

Victor was patting his shoulder as Hamish said, "It's alright. I'm just tired after the shock and all the formalities."

The service was soothing and they all relaxed.

"Come home with us for lunch." Katrina was insistent. She was sick of her social life around the hotel. It was so nice to ease off and talk to friends.

Hamish was certainly looking better and the afternoon passed pleasantly.

"I must go now," he said.

The last ferry left at 4 p.m. on Sundays and he had to be in Edinburgh to start his new job.

"I'll be in touch," he said as he ran for the ferry and Lorna Jean walked slowly home.

Chapter 18

It was the end of the school year and Lorna Jean had made no plans.

She was just about to go to bed when the phone rang.

"It's Hamish."

"Where are you?" she asked, her heart skipping a beat at the sound of the voice of the man she couldn't dismiss from her mind.

"In an Edinburgh hotel at an end-of-term dinner. Could you meet me in Oban tomorrow? There are lots of things I'd like to discuss with you."

"Such as?"

"Ah, that would be telling."

She dressed carefully for the meeting and so, she noticed, had he as she slipped her arm through his.

They were having tea in the Singing Kettle when he took the jeweller's box from his pocket. He slid it across the table. "Will you marry me?"

She giggled nervously and said "The last man went down on his bended knee."

"And look where that got you!" He smiled. "Try it on for size." It was slightly on the large size. "I'll get it sized, that is if you intend to keep it."

"And answer your proposal? The answer is 'Yes', the question is when?"

"In three weeks' time."

"My God!"

"There won't be time for either of us to bail out. No giving back presents or people being disappointed. This will be for us — a civil ceremony. We won't even know the witnesses, not even Victor or Katrina will know our secret until the knot is tied. I'll pick you up after the prize-giving and we'll say we are going on holiday. Then we'll make for the Gretna Hotel and make all the arrangements."

Lorna Jean opened her purse and took out Crawford's ring. "I'll give you this for my ring size," she said.

His face was a study in expression.

"Once yours is on my finger, I never want to see that one again. Do what you want with it. Pawn it, give it to a charity shop — anything — it's up to you."

He looked worried. "It's a very valuable ring," he pointed out.

"What he paid for it was only a fraction of the money I lost in the wedding preparations." Lorna Jean's voice was bitter.

"Well, if you say so." He slipped the ring into his wallet and they made the final plans.

Lorna Jean escaped from the island with comparative ease, and soon they were covering the miles that would lead them to the happy ending.

The receptionist raised her eyebrows when Hamish booked two single rooms.

"We're just an old-fashioned couple about to be married and I don't want to see my bride in all her finery before the wedding."

They went to the first room. Hamish opened the door, then took the single key of the adjoining one and opened the connecting door. "First choice to the bride," he said.

Lorna Jean giggled. "Have you eloped before?"

"No! But I once stayed here on a coach tour. The old man in the next room snored every night."

"A likely story," Lorna Jean said as she started to unpack to the distant sound of bagpipes.

"I've ordered that for us," Hamish assured her. "And one of my rugby pals, Ernest Deans and his wife are coming over from Carlisle to be our witnesses. I was the best man at their wedding. Beryl, his wife, will help you to dress, and there's a special meal laid on for the four of us." He looked so relaxed.

The dividing door was locked the night before the wedding. Beryl was coming for the night and would be next door. Hamish was with Ernest in Carlisle and would be at the ceremony at twelve noon.

"What have you got that all the others who tried and failed don't have?" Beryl teased.

"I just happened to be there at the psychological moment." Lorna Jean was stepping into the smart ivory silk suit and pinning on the tiny white veil with the single white rose to keep it firmly attached. The small white pouch handbag had a matching rose.

Beryl, who was blonde and fashionable, wore a deep blue dress with a red rose in her hair.

"I just can't believe this is happening," Lorna Jean said.

"I wish I had had the sense to go for something like this," Beryl said wistfully. "Mine cost thousands and led to civil war in the family."

They went in to the sound of the piper and tourists from the coaches cheering them on.

There was love in Hamish's eyes as she walked to his side and they made their vows.

The hotel chef had made a bride's cake and packed it to be taken home. There were four sizeable pieces for the four of them to have with the toast, which was Asti Spumante, Hamish's favourite wine.

"That's the most enjoyable day I've had for ages," Ernest said and he really meant it.

"We'll keep in touch" they said as Hamish drove the car from the car park.

"Here's to us," he said as they took the road to the Lakes.

The first night of the honeymoon was sheer bliss. "Well worth waiting for," he said as they lay, satisfied, in each other's arms.

The sun shone and they sailed on the lake, and took mountain paths for glorious views.

At night in the hotel they met the most interesting people.
"You're looking so well," Hamish said.
"I feel as if I'm being introduced to a whole new way of life," Lorna Jean observed as they sipped the creamy coffee and crunched fresh ginger biscuits.
"Tomorrow, Wordsworth's cottage," Hamish suggested. "It's time we had a little bit of culture."

The guide in the cottage was one of the most interesting Lorna Jean had ever listened to and she was hanging to every word he said, realizing meanwhile that his eyes were fixed on Hamish. As the crowd melted away, the guide rushed up to them.

"Scotso!" They were hugging, shaking hands. Then the guide said "What the hell are you doing here?"

Hamish chuckled. "You'll never believe it old boy. We're here on honeymoon — meet the wife."

Charles was really astonished. "I'm off duty now. Let's go to the gingerbread café and celebrate." He took Lorna Jean's arm. Hamish trailed behind.

"Sorry it can't be anything stronger. We're both driving."

He ordered tea and gingerbread, then excused himself.

"Is he an old friend?" Lorna Jean was intrigued.

"We shared a room at university. He's doing an extra degree and obviously working to pay the fees."

Suddenly, Charles reappeared, helping the waitress to carry the treat. He put down the heavy teapot and placed a small, beautifully-wrapped parcel on the table beside Lorna Jean. "A small token of esteem," he said.

The men talked while she refilled cups, cut thick wedges of gingerbread, so happy for Hamish to meet his college friend.

Then he looked at his watch. "Good heavens!" He was standing up, shaking hands and saying how lovely it was to have met them. "Sorry to leave you. I'm due to take a school party round the cottage in quarter of an hour."

There was still some tea in the pot. Hamish went to the counter and bought two custard tarts. "I always know I'm in England when I eat custard tarts," he said.

Lorna Jean phoned her mother on the last day of the honeymoon.

"Married?" she yelled over the telephone.

"Yes, we eloped to Gretna Green."

At that point, she banged down the receiver.

Hamish's mother was similarly displeased.

"Ah well, we've done our duty. Don't worry, they'll come round, if only out of sheer curiosity." He was probably right, Lorna Jean reckoned. All that mattered was that the honeymoon was magic and that she was no longer a woman alone.

"You sneaky devils," Katrina said as they dropped in at the hotel with the news.

"You should talk." Hamish was laughing as a bottle of champagne was opened.

"So, what happens now about your career and the cottage?" Katrina sounded anxious.

"It's all fixed. We stay together at the cottage until Hamish takes over at the university in October. I'll work my notice at the school, then we'll go to live in his Edinburgh flat and come back to the cottage for holidays and weekends."

"Isn't it a God's blessing that your mother bought you a double bed." Katrina loved it when Lorna Jean blushed.

"She did not buy it for that. The idea was for my father and her to take over when I was away on holiday."

They finished the meal and went home, Lorna Jean to write her resignation, Hamish to tackle the neglected garden.

"This is the life," he declared and sealed it with a kiss.